ALL I NEED

HAVEN'S BAY HOLIDAY SERIES

J.H. CROIX

To letting go.

Sign up for my newsletter for information on new releases & get a FREE copy of one of my books!

http://jhcroixauthor.com/subscribe/

Follow me!
jhcroix@jhcroix.com
https://amazon.com/author/jhcroix
https://www.bookbub.com/authors/j-h-croix
https://www.facebook.com/jhcroix
https://www.instagram.com/jhcroix/

Reader's Note: a short version of this story (17,000-ish words) was released as part of a time-limited free anthology, Holiday Ever After, in Nov/Dec 2019. That anthology was only available for a limited time. This expanded version is over 45,000 words.

Chapter One

SASHA

My headlights offered a narrow path of visibility through the falling snow. Fortunately, my little SUV navigated easily through the roughly six inches of snow piled up on the driveway. I also knew this driveway was a straight shot to the house from the road.

"Hello, Haven's Bay," I murmured to myself.

My dog's tail thumped against the seat, and her furry face appeared in the rearview mirror. "We're almost there, Matilda." Her tail thumped in reply.

Although Boston, where I lived, was roughly four hours away from my old hometown, I'd only sporadically come back to the town in Maine where I grew up. The few visits I'd had over the years had been very brief.

The stately house came into view. It stood tall in the snowy darkness with my headlights illuminating the front steps. There wasn't a single light on. It somehow made sense that my return to Haven's Bay would be dark, snowy, and without anyone to welcome me.

The sound of my tires was muffled as they rolled through the snow, creating a little path in my rearview mirror. I came to a quiet stop. I didn't wait because it was cold, and I needed to get inside and turn the heat on.

I left my headlights on, let Matilda out, and hurried toward the front steps. Blessedly, I was wearing a pair of practical black leather boots. Even then, the snow was cold over the tops. Light and fluffy, it slid down into my boots, dampening my socks as I dashed along the path lit by my headlights and up the stairs. I stumbled slightly, but I managed not to fall.

My friend Thea had mailed me the house key, and I fished it out of my pocket, fumbling to find the lock on the heavy front door. In another moment, I finally got the key in and turned it. I pushed the door open, the sound of my footsteps echoing in the tiled entryway.

I reached for the light switch to one side of the door. "Hello," I whispered to myself as I pushed the switch up. Darkness reigned as nothing flickered on.

"Oh, shit." My muttered imprecation echoed in the dark foyer.

This grand old colonial home belonged to my closest childhood friend and her siblings. They hadn't lived here in years either, but they occasionally used it for vacations. Although it had been years since I'd been here, I recalled how it looked. I was standing inside a two-story foyer with a curved staircase along one side with a hallway straight ahead. Along one side of the hall lay the kitchen and the dining room, while what was once a formal parlor room was on the other side.

Despite its familiarity, the entire house now felt spooky and dark and decidedly cold. "Fuck."

Thea must not've known the power was off. I didn't know what to do. Should I call her? Double fuck. I hadn't brought my phone in. It was sitting in my warm SUV, plugged into the charger.

I closed the heavy front door behind me, leaning against it and taking a deep breath. So much for my escape to the Maine coast.

I unclipped Matilda's leash. She was going

to sniff like crazy. Her claws skittered on the floor as she dashed forward. She was sniffing so hard that the sound of it echoed in the quiet space. If a serial killer was hiding somewhere in this house, she would find them.

Taking a deep breath, I pushed away from the door. My eyes had adjusted to the darkness, and I could make out the shape of the staircase and the banister I used to slide down with Thea when we were little girls. It was a most excellent banister for that, wide and glossy. The curve made it fun.

Once upon a time, we'd dragged out a mattress and put it at the bottom. We'd landed in a giggling heap. Those were the days. Our childhoods were anything but perfect, but our friendship had been just about flawless. We didn't see each other much anymore, but we stayed in touch. Thea was one of *those* friends, the kind I could call no matter how much time had elapsed, and we could fall into a conversation as if we'd just spoken the day before.

When my teenage daughter had begged to go on a ski trip with her aunt for the holidays, I had hemmed and hawed because it would be my first Christmas without her. As a single parent who'd become a mother at the scandalous age of sixteen, it was hard to let go. Thea had told me it was the perfect time for a vacation and some time to myself. I couldn't argue against that, and I didn't want to be the kind of mom who clung too hard. My daughter, Quinn, was on her way to Vermont, and I had a week here on the windswept coast of Maine.

Thea had said, "It'll be perfect. You can have the house to yourself and finally enjoy the pretty views again."

At the moment, it wasn't looking so perfect. I had no power and wasn't quite sure what to do. Luckily, it wasn't actually Christmas. It was a week before, so I had time to salvage this.

I decided to venture outside to get my phone and use it as a flashlight. It had one of those flashlight apps on it, although I hadn't ever imagined needing it.

I could still hear Matilda sniffing about, so I stepped out quickly, dashing through the snow and following the tracks I'd created before. I grabbed my down coat out of the passenger seat and my phone before rushing back in. I knew where the fuses were in the basement. I also knew this house didn't have one of those scary old basements.

The year before I was banished from town because I got pregnant, Thea's parents had upgraded the basement. Matilda followed me as I carefully descended the stairs in the darkness, the carpeted stairs quiet under my footsteps. Memory was a funny thing. It kind of surprised me that I knew the old fuse box was in the back corner of the basement by the door that led to a set of stairs and another door that went outside.

Shining my phone flashlight on the fuse box, I scanned the rows of fuses. As far as I could tell, they were all on. My hopes for power tonight were dimming.

Turning, I made my way back up the stairs with Matilda bounding ahead of me. Her claws clicked on the hardwood flooring once she crested the top stair. I closed the basement door behind me and stood still in the middle of the hallway, wondering what to do.

Just then, I heard a soft click, followed immediately by Matilda's sharp bark.

"Who the hell are you?" The voice was male, with the words delivered in a low, commanding tone.

Great. There was no power, I was alone with my exuberantly friendly dog, and now there was a strange man here. I was pretty sure I was being held at gunpoint in the dark. I was also getting cold.

Chapter Two

NOAH

The woman squeaked. Her dog started sniffing my feet, its tail thumping my legs as it circled me excitedly. After its initial bark, this dog didn't appear inclined to be intimidating.

"You know, it's bad form to bring your dog to a break-in," I commented.

Even though I didn't know who this woman was, I was pretty sure she wasn't a threat. But she *was* in my family's old home, deserted and quiet in the darkness. Considering that the driveway was long enough that the front of the house wasn't visible from the road, it didn't really matter that she'd left her headlights shining on the house outside.

Maybe having my gun out was overkill,

but then, when I came into the back of the house, I didn't know she had a dog, nor that she was a woman. I watched her hands slowly lift in the shadowy hallway.

"My hands are up," she said in a shaky voice. "I promise I didn't break-in. I have a key. Thea gave it to me."

The second she said my little sister's name, I lowered my gun and tucked it into my holster. I shouldn't have even been wearing my holster, but old habits die hard and all that. I'd left at the end of a long day at work in the FBI in Boston and come straight here. "Who are you?"

"Sasha, Sasha Hilts."

"Sasha?"

"I think it's only fair you tell me who you are," Sasha returned.

"It's Noah, Noah Tate. You know, Thea's older brother."

Sasha let out a giant sigh that echoed in the hallway. Her dog was still circling me, and I leaned down to stroke the dog's head. "What's your dog's name?"

"Matilda."

"Hey, Matilda," I said conversationally as I scratched behind her ears. Matilda loved that and leaned into my hand.

"There's no power," Sasha announced.

"There's power. I just have to turn it on outside."

"Oh. Well, that's good. What are you doing here?"

Sasha followed me as I turned and walked toward the back of the house. I went through the archway that led into the kitchen and straight to the screen door at the back. I'd left it open when I came inside.

"Do you need help?" Sasha asked as we stopped at the doorway.

"Nah. Give me a sec."

The snow was still falling as I tromped through it to the outside power box about ten feet away from the kitchen doorway. Using a small flashlight I'd slipped in my pocket for the sole purpose of doing this, I held it in my teeth and quickly turned on the main switch to the house. Since my siblings and I, who shared our childhood home, were rarely here, we always turned off the power outside at the main circuit. We also drained the pipes and turned off the water main. I'd turn the water on once we had some light.

In a few seconds, the hallway light Sasha must've switched on when she came through the front turned on, along with the kitchen lights. Sasha held the door open for me as I walked through and closed it behind me. I knocked the snow off my boots. Matilda was busy sniffing around the edges of the kitchen.

I lifted my head, and my eyes collided with Sasha's. I hadn't seen Sasha in years. She was one of Thea's closest childhood friends and four years younger than me, just like my sister. She'd been cute when she was a teenager, but now, she literally grabbed my breath and snatched it right out of my chest.

Her dark hair was pulled up in a messy bun with loose tendrils dangling around her face. Her cheeks were pink from the cold, and her green eyes were bright as she stared back at me.

I gave myself a mental kick. "Well, long time, no see," I finally said.

Her eyes searched my face. "It's definitely been a while."

After a beat, I noticed she had her arms wrapped tightly around her waist and was shivering slightly.

"Let me make sure the boiler is up and running. We need some heat, and I'll turn on the water."

Striding past her, I crossed into the hallway and down the basement stairs. Matilda followed me, with Sasha coming as well. I turned on the water main and flicked on the switch to fire up the boiler. Like the power, we turned it off when we weren't here.

After a minute, I nodded as I heard the sound of it starting up. Turning, I looked at Sasha again, startled at the jolt that sizzled through me.

"Let's get a fire started in the living room and kitchen. It's probably gonna take a few hours for the house to warm up. I had no idea you'd be here," I called over my shoulder as I walked up the stairs.

"Obviously, I didn't know you were going to be here," Sasha replied. "Thea offered to let me stay here for a week. I guess I need to make other arrangements."

We crested the top of the stairs, and she followed me into the kitchen. This home was old enough that we actually had a freaking fireplace in here. When I was growing up, my parents had updated it with a wood stove insert for efficiency. This, in addition to the large fireplace in the living room, would do a nice job of throwing off some heat.

"No need to make other arrangements," I said as I began to gather wood stacked neatly in a rack right beside the stove. I presumed my older brother, Dallas, who had been here last Christmas, had enough sense to leave the wood behind. He was that kind of guy, always organized and planning ahead.

"Are you sure? Are other people coming?"

"Nobody else will be here until next weekend. Lord knows, there's plenty of room."

When I straightened, Sasha was chewing on her bottom lip. Fuck me. She had a mouth made for sin. Her lips were plump and full, and a little dimple was right in the center of her bottom lip. Her teeth dented the smooth pink surface as she stared at me.

"Are you sure?" she repeated.

"Absolutely."

At that moment, her stomach growled. She slapped her palm over it, her cheeks flushing pink. This woman was a walking distraction. In the corner of my mind, I wondered if it was crazy that I'd just told her it was no problem for her to stay here. But she was one of my sister's best friends, so I wasn't about to kick her out in the snowy darkness.

"Hungry?" I asked dryly.

"Apparently," she said with a sheepish smile.

"I picked up a pizza on the way through town. I'll help you unload what you have, and then we can heat it."

———

By the time Sasha set the empty paper plate on the coffee table and leaned back into the couch cushions, the living room was warm and cozy. The snow was still falling outside with gusts of wind buffeting the house while we ate. She'd fed Matilda in the kitchen, and Matilda had trotted into the living room with us and was currently napping in front of the fireplace .

"So what are you doing here a week before Christmas?" Sasha asked.

Thus far, we had covered the basics. We'd investigated the options for bedrooms. Only one room actually had a bed in it. My two brothers, my sister, and I were slowly getting the house furnished after almost losing it in a legal mess our father created, but the house had been stripped of everything by the time Dallas had managed to save it from the creditors.

I'd insisted Sasha take the room with the bed, and I would sleep on the couch. Maybe we didn't have the whole place furnished yet, but Thea and I had picked out this cushy sectional last year. I had no worries about sleeping comfortably on it.

After I'd helped Sasha carry her things in,

she'd insisted on helping me with mine. All the while, I managed to notice far too much of Sasha. She was wearing jeans, and the fabric hugged her lush bottom. My palms itched to slide over her curves and savor their feel.

Considering she thought no one would be here, I knew she wasn't dressed for my attention. Unfortunately for me, and decidedly inconveniently, Sasha in jeans and a faded V-neck T-shirt did nothing but rev my body's engine.

I remembered Sasha being attractive before, but I was four years ahead of her in school, so I didn't pay too much attention. Now, she was fucking gorgeous in a sort of messy, haphazard way.

"Noah?" she prompted.

Oh, right. We were having a conversation. "I needed a break from work. You know I work at the FBI, right?"

Sasha nodded. "Yes. You and Dallas. For a while, Thea thought she might do the same, but she decided it was probably more stress than she preferred."

I chuckled with a bitter twist in my gut. I was too close to that stress these days. "No, she wouldn't have appreciated the stress. I like my job, but I needed a break, so that's why I'm here."

Sasha nodded and brushed a loose hair off the side of her neck, drawing my eyes there. My brain went to another place it wasn't supposed to go, wondering what she would taste like. I wanted to nibble on that sensitive skin and see how she reacted.

"Noah?" Her prompt punctured my inappropriate train of thought again. While nothing was technically wrong with me thinking my sister's now thirty-year-old best friend was hot, somehow, I didn't think that was where Sasha's mind was at the moment.

Chapter Three

SASHA

Noah gave his head a slight shake, lifting his eyes to meet mine again. Oh wow. I'd forgotten how intense Noah Tate's gaze was. His chocolate-brown eyes matched his hair perfectly. When I was old enough to notice guys in high school, he'd been hard not to notice, yet I doubted I even registered on his radar back then. But as one of the older brothers of my closest friend, he'd been the star of a few fantasies. Luckily for me, I'd been a sensible girl until that one time when I was spectacularly not.

But me being sensible or not had nothing to do with Noah. I just had enough sense to realize he was four years older than me and would never bother with me, so I hadn't let myself get too hung up on him. Of course, I did wonder why I'd never gotten hung up on Ian, who was the youngest of Thea's brothers and only two years older than us. All her brothers were handsome, but I'd only fantasized about Noah back then. Seeing him years later in the flesh was almost overwhelming.

The years had been kind to Noah. His once boyish good looks were honed and sharpened. He had a jaw sharp enough to cut glass and sculpted cheekbones with an aquiline nose. His intense dark gaze added a dash of intimidation. I giggled, thinking about how he'd pulled a gun on me in the hallway. I would've been terrified if I'd had much time to think about it or seen what I imagined the look in his eyes had been at that moment.

One of his brows rose in a slash while one corner of his mouth kicked up in a bemused grin. That look sent my belly wild, butterflies tickling as they spun inside.

"What's so funny?" he asked.

I shrugged. "I was just thinking it was probably good I didn't see your face when you pulled a gun on me earlier. It probably would've terrified me."

His grin stretched to the other corner of

his mouth, and my pulse cheered, taking off in a mad dash. "Sorry about that. I honestly had no idea who was here. I didn't figure it was all that bad because most burglars don't bring their dogs, but my habits kicked in."

"Are you carrying your gun now?" I couldn't help but ask.

He shook his head. "Nah. I put it away. I literally came straight here from our offices in Boston. I know Thea offered you the house, but what are you doing here all alone? You have a daughter, right?"

Even though Noah had graduated and left town by the time my life became the mini-teenage drama of Haven's Bay High School, there was no way he hadn't heard the whole story. I got pregnant when I was fifteen and had a baby when I was sixteen. And—*oh!*—what a scandal it had been.

"Quinn's on a ski trip with her aunt for Christmas. It's my first whole week without her. I needed a change of pace, so Thea offered me the house. If you prefer for me to get a hotel, I'll find something tomorrow. I hate to intrude. I don't think Thea knew you were planning to be here."

My body was going flat-out haywire around Noah. Between my pulse, these waves of heat rolling through me, and my belly working on some kind of gymnastics routine, I didn't even know what to think. But now, genuine worry and anxiety spun into the mix, and it wasn't a good combination. I didn't want to drive back to Boston because I really needed a change of scenery just to reset and get my bearings. I also didn't have money for a hotel. This wasn't working out how I had hoped, but I *really* didn't want to impose on Noah.

"Thea definitely had no idea I'd be here. Because I didn't tell her. I made the decision in my head this morning," he said, tapping his temple before leaning over to lift his beer off the coffee table.

"You sure came prepared," I observed, my eyes drawn to the motion of his throat as he tilted his head back.

Sweet hell. Apparently, I had a thing for his throat, and his wrist. Watching the flex of it, I let my gaze linger on his fingers as they slid along the bottle when he lowered it. I wondered what his hands would feel like on me.

Besides my one and only teenage scandal, I'd lived a rather staid and decidedly boring life since then. Being a young single mother didn't lend itself to the dating world. I was always scrambling to make ends meet, just to keep my head above water. Half the time, I felt like I was treading water madly only to slip below the surface every so often. Most of the guys around my age were shocked—*shocked*, I tell you—that I had a teenage daughter. They weren't even ready to think about having a baby, much less navigating the treacherous waters of parenting a teenager, especially one who wasn't theirs.

When you had a child, dating necessitated brutal honesty up front. Because I didn't have time to waste at all, much less get to know someone with zero interest in dating someone with a child. It wasn't like I went into dating looking for Quinn's imaginary stepfather. I just couldn't imagine putting time in with someone who wasn't into kids. Long story short, I didn't get much action. At all.

Maybe all that lack of sex was what had me so tied up in knots over Noah. This was probably the closest thing I'd had to a date in years, even though he had no idea, and that was crazy thinking.

He chuckled. "I stopped at the grocery store when I passed through town. Got a pizza to go and some beer and wine. I picked up bagels and cream cheese for breakfast. I grabbed some eggs too, although I have no idea what I'll do with them."

I grinned back at him, and maybe I was seriously out of practice, but I could've sworn for just a second I saw a flare go off in his eyes. Maybe that, or perhaps I was losing my mind. Sexy was not the word that came to mind when men knew anything about my life.

"I can whip up some omelets. Even plain egg omelets are good if you have a few spices knocking around the kitchen."

"I got cheese and coffee and cream too. I thought ahead," he added, giving me a quick wink.

My belly did another spin.

"To reiterate, you're not imposing. This is a giant house." He gestured expansively with his hand around the large living room. The ceilings were tall in this old house, so every room felt spacious, even the old servants' rooms on the uppermost floor.

This house was once owned by some crazy-wealthy family a few centuries ago. They had paid staff and everything back in the day. I remember being excited to spend the night here when I was a kid. Thea and I would stay upstairs in the old servants' bedrooms. They were also sizable rooms. The slanted ceilings of the upper floor just didn't create as much airy space as the rest of the house.

"If you're sure. If you change your mind in the morning when you're feeling saner and it's not snowing and windy, just let me know," I finally said.

Noah held my gaze for several long beats, and my stomach went back to its gymnastics routine while my pulse raced. "I'm not changing my mind, Sasha. So back to you. Your daughter's on a ski trip, and it's your first vacation without her. Seriously?"

I arched my brows and pursed my lips. "Yes, Noah. I'm a single mother. I love it, and I wouldn't change it, but it doesn't give me much time to myself, much less the funds for many vacations."

He nodded slowly. "I wasn't here when it all went down, but if I recall, Thea told me your parents kicked you out. Did they really?"

I nodded. "They sure did. It's okay. I stumbled a few times, but I landed on my feet. Family isn't always great."

"You don't have to tell me. You know what happened with my family."

While I recalled Noah's mother had been lovely—always warm and kind—it was no secret in town that their father had been a wealthy asshole. Their mother had passed away, and their father was in jail. He'd wanted to make more money and did so by breaking the law.

I winced slightly. "I do. I'm sorry about your mother." As soon as I said that, I realized the last time I'd seen him was probably at his mother's funeral.

He inclined his head in acknowledgment. "So your parents kicked you out, and then what?" he asked quickly, making it clear he didn't want to dwell on his mother. I didn't blame him because I imagined he missed her. I knew Thea did.

"I got knocked up, got kicked out, and believe it or not, I ended up in this program for young teenage mothers. The night my parents kicked me out, I actually came to spend the night with Thea. You were off in college. Your mom called somebody in Boston, somebody she knew. The next day, she gave me a ride down there. She told me I could've stayed with Thea, but your father wouldn't allow it."

Noah interjected, "Of course not. Fucking asshole."

When my eyes widened, he caught my look and shrugged. "I'm all about being direct about what happened. My dad's an asshole. It's okay. I miss my mom, and we were blessed to have her. I didn't get a full winning hand when it came to family, but I got two out of three."

"Two out of three?" I prompted, not understanding what he meant.

"An awesome mom and siblings I love."

"Oh," I said softly. "I guess I got zero out of three."

I didn't even feel bitter about it. Because despite money being tight and my nonexistent love life, I had a pretty good life, and I loved my daughter dearly.

Noah leaned over and lifted his bottle of beer. Once again, I watched the flex of his throat when he swallowed and wondered what his skin tasted like. He set the now-empty beer bottle down, giving me a considering look. "All right, three out of four then. I wasn't counting right."

"What do you mean by that?"

"I got an awesome mom, my great siblings, and life's all right for me, even with a little stress. So you got two out of four."

"How do you figure?" I pressed.

"Because you're awesome. You're Thea's best friend, and she says you're a true sister since she didn't get one. You got thrown a curveball in high school, but it sounds like you're doing all right, and you have a kid who I'm guessing you love." At my nod, he flashed a quick grin. "I never knew my mom helped you. What did she do?"

"I don't know how your mom knew her, but she knew a woman who did fundraising for some program in Boston. Your mom took me to meet her, and that woman set me up with this program. They had housing, and I got to finish high school and do job training too. By the time I left, I had two years of college credits. Then I got a scholarship as part of a work-study program."

"In all that time, you knew you wanted to keep the baby?"

That was the first stutter in his questioning. I sensed his hesitance.

"Sort of, but it wasn't easy to decide." I rubbed my fingers along the edge of the fuzzy knitted throw draped over my lap. "The program supported us with whatever we wanted to do. It wasn't like one of those homes trying to make you have the baby. They set me up with a counselor and sent me to educational seminars on parenting, adoption, and even abortion. I wasn't sure what to do, but I was already four months along when I got there. I actually thought I was going to give her up for adoption." I wrinkled my nose, twisting my lips a little sadly. "Even though I wanted to keep her, I thought that was best because I didn't have a lot of money. But when I had Quinn and held her, I just couldn't do it. I felt really bad about it. Fortunately, the way they had the adoption program set up, you weren't supposed to meet the prospective parents until after you had the baby. About two months later, one of the other girls in the program did go through with an adoption, so the same family adopted her baby. It was weird feeling bad about that, and I was so relieved it worked out for them."

Noah stared at me intently and then nodded. "Damn. You are one strong woman. I don't know how you did it."

"With a lot of help. It all started because your mom made a phone call and knew somebody. Life is funny like that."

"Mom was adopted. She donated money to stuff like that all the time."

"She was? She didn't tell me that."

"She was pretty private about it. She loved her parents, but it was a thing for her, to make sure mothers had the support they needed. She found her bio mom later, and it turns out, that her mom was young and totally overwhelmed. It worked out differently for you. So yeah, two out of four."

I rolled my eyes. "No need to count. I *am* doing okay. Quinn's an amazing daughter, and I love her to pieces. Honestly, it played out the way it was going to play out. My parents were never that supportive. They lost their shit when I got pregnant."

"What about now?"

"They both died. My mom and I sort of reconciled. Dad had liver cancer. Not a shocker because he was a functioning alcoholic his whole adult life. My mom reached out to me. I went to see him, and it was okay. I wanted Quinn to meet my mom, so that was good. She passed away only two years ago after she had a stroke. That was it."

"Did they leave anything for you?"

I shook my head. "My parents did okay, but my dad blew through their retirement money. He got sick before they were old enough to be on Medicare and didn't have health insurance. My mom used what little money they had left to pay off his medical bills, and then she was gone. Thank goodness the hospital couldn't chase me for anything they owed because Lord knows what charges they racked up in the end."

"Wow. You've just been making it work all

by yourself," Noah said softly. "I'd love to meet your daughter sometime."

"Well, if you don't get sick of me this week, we can get lunch or something in Boston." It was strange to realize we'd both been living in the same city and hadn't seen each other in all these years.

"I'm not going to get sick of you. This house is big enough to hide from each other. Should we meet for coffee in the kitchen tomorrow morning?"

I laughed. "Of course."

"Let me check to ensure that the bedroom's warm enough."

A few minutes later, I was standing in the bedroom, the one and only room with a bed in the house, and it suddenly felt small despite being large and spacious. Noah had one hand curled on the doorframe above as he looked at me. "Are you good for the night?"

His stance was relaxed, but his shirt had ridden up slightly with his arm lifted, revealing a strip of skin above his jeans. That, and one side of the well-defined V that disappeared behind his waistband.

When he arched a brow in question at my silence, I managed to nod, trying to get a breath in, but my lungs were doing a poor job. "All set," I squeaked.

With a quick smile, he left, closing the door behind him. I listened to his footsteps retreat down the hallway as I sank my hips on the bed and wondered how to wrestle my body under control. If this was how I reacted to Noah every time I got close to him, it was going to be a long week.

Chapter Four

NOAH

A drop of maple syrup glistening at the corner of Sasha's mouth caught my eyes. My body tightened, and fiery electricity sizzled through my veins. Matters were promptly made worse when her pink tongue darted out to catch that drop of maple syrup.

She finished chewing and set down her fork. "That was yummy."

Sherry Levesque stopped by our table, smiling fondly at us. She and her husband owned Bay Bistro, the café where we'd stopped for breakfast. "I am so glad you both came in this morning." Her gaze lingered on Sasha. "It's lovely to see you back in town, dear. How long will you be here?"

Sasha's smile was friendly but careful. It

wasn't that I hadn't known her story, but the implications of how it must've been for her had hit me hard last night. I sensed she wasn't sure what anyone in Haven's Bay thought of her. Being well-versed in dealing with drama as a part of a family that had its own share of scandal in this small town, I felt intensely protective. That feeling tangling up in my raw lust for her was a confusing mix, to say the least.

"At least for the week. After that, I need to be back at work in Boston," Sasha replied.

Sherry nodded. "Of course. How is your daughter?"

"She's great. Thanks for asking."

Sherry's attention was drawn away when another customer gestured for her. Glancing back, she cast us another warm smile. "You let me know if you need anything else, okay?"

After Sherry hurried off, Sasha lifted her coffee and took a swallow. This morning, she dressed unassumingly again. She wore fleece leggings with an open blouse over a fitted tank top. She'd shed her bulky down jacket once we got inside.

After making a quick pot of coffee out at the house, we'd decided to come out for breakfast when I discovered the limited options for pots and pans in the kitchen. When my father lost almost everything, the only thing my eldest brother had been able to keep for our family was the old family home. That said, somewhere along the way, just about everything in it had been auctioned off.

Collectively, we were gradually refurbishing the house. None of us lived here, though, so it was happening in fits and starts.

Bay Bistro was a favorite local café that served brunch, lunch, and dinner. Emile and Sherry Levesque, an old Haven's Bay family, owned it as well as several other businesses in town, including the main grocery store and another restaurant.

"Has your daughter ever been to Haven's Bay?" I asked.

Sasha nodded. "A few times. Though she never even stayed in the house where I grew up. My parents sold it."

I held her gaze for a beat before commenting, "I hate thinking about how everything went for you."

"There's no need. Like I told you last night, I landed on my feet. We're doing fine, better than fine. Quinn's a straight-A high school student. She has friends, and hopefully, she'll be off to college in a few years. I can't even believe that's almost here."

"I bet not. I don't even have a baby yet. I certainly can't imagine having a child about to go off to college in a few years."

Sasha rolled her eyes, her lips twisting. "Yeah, most people anywhere close to my age can't imagine it. It's great for dating," she said, sarcasm lacing her tone.

I cocked my head to the side. "What do you mean?"

"Trying to date as a single parent is hard enough, but it tends to raise eyebrows when people realize I'm thirty-one and have a fifteen-year-old daughter."

"What the hell is wrong with that?"

She lifted a hand, letting it fall to the table. "I don't know. I've given up on dating. It's not like I have much time, as it is."

"You didn't mention what you do for work," I commented. It was crazy Sasha hadn't been snapped up by some man intelligent enough to realize she was not only smart and strong but also fucking beautiful and sexy as hell.

"I'm a paralegal, and I lucked out because I love my job. I had an internship at a smaller but very well-established law firm in Boston. The woman who I interned for offered me a job, and I've been there ever since. The pay is good, and I love her. I work my ass off, but that's fine. I've never minded doing hard work."

"It's a pretty sweet deal having a good boss and doing a job you enjoy when it comes to work."

"Exactly."

At that moment, a couple passed by our table. The woman glanced our way and then did a double-take when she saw Sasha. Sasha glanced up, her eyes turning steely, and her lips pressing in a line.

After the couple moved out of earshot, I asked, "Who is that?" I vaguely recognized them, but I couldn't quite place them.

"Friends of my father's. She used to be his secretary. I was never a fan. Even though it's old news that I got pregnant in high school, it's strange to be back here. When I left, I felt like everybody thought I was a whore."

"Fuck them all," I said flatly. "That's ridiculous. Not to mention, what did everybody think of the father?"

Sasha's gaze hardened. "That he wasn't responsible. It was Jonathon Smith, and his parents were horrified. It was my own mistake. He's never had anything to do with her or paid one penny of child support. His sister is the only one I've had contact with in that family. She reached out after college. She's not close to her parents, and she's the one who took Quinn on the ski trip. She lives in Western Mass and stops by whenever she's in Boston. Years later, after calling me a whore to my face when I was fifteen, Jonathon's mother reached out and wanted to meet Quinn, but she didn't want me to be there. I refused."

"I don't blame you," I said firmly, that sense of protectiveness sharpening inside me. "She doesn't need to meet people who treated you that way and weren't there for you in any way."

"I actually asked Quinn what she wanted," Sasha said, grimacing slightly. "Because if it was something she wanted, I would've let her meet her. She didn't. Maybe that'll change, and I'll have to figure out what to do. She's old enough now that all I can do is try to support what she wants and hope no one hurts her."

Later that afternoon, after Sasha and I had gone our separate ways, I returned to the house. I'd headed to a town nearby to buy a few more pots and pans for the kitchen. As I rolled to a stop in the circular driveway, I glanced over to see Sasha in the middle of shoveling the front porch and stairs.

Tall and rectangular, my family's old colonial-style home was situated on a bluff looking out over the ocean. The front of the home had a porch that ran the length of the house. Other than a small arching overhang above the door, it was otherwise uncovered, including the stairs.

I climbed out of the car, calling over, "You don't have to shovel."

Sasha glanced up, casting me a quick smile. "It's the least I can do. I don't mind shoveling."

Reaching the bottom step, she quickly scooped off the last bit of snow and then walked toward my car. "Do you need help?"

She stopped in front of me, and I glanced down. Her down jacket was unzipped, revealing a denim button-down shirt over her tank top. Her breasts rose and fell with every breath she took. My hands itched to touch her. Her cheeks were flushed pink, and her hair was pulled up into a messy ponytail with loose tendrils framing her face. Without thinking, I lifted a hand and brushed a few wayward locks out of the way, tucking them behind her ear. The pull to dip my head and kiss her was so strong that it took an act of sheer will not to do it.

Her eyes held mine under the bright winter sun. I thought I saw an answering flare of desire in her gaze. "What did you get?"

It took me a moment to gather my focus. "Some more stuff for the kitchen. I actually contemplated getting some furniture, but then I decided I didn't want to take on that project today. I also got us more groceries."

"I can reimburse you," she said.

"No."

She let out a huff of a laugh. "No?"

"That's right. No."

She pursed her lips. "I'll reimburse Thea then."

"My sister's not going to take money from you."

Sasha cuffed me lightly on the shoulder as she turned away and propped the shovel against the railing on the stairs. Of course, my eyes went right to her bottom. She was not short on curves. If I thought her jeans did her sweet body justice, her fleece leggings were even worse, outlining every inch of her generous hips.

Turning back, she asked, "What can I carry?"

We got everything unloaded, and then I found myself in the kitchen after we let Matilda outside to run around. I looked down into Sasha's eyes.

The need to kiss her felt like a whip lashing at my back. She was standing right there, her hand resting on the kitchen counter as she drew her tongue along the spoon she'd just dipped in honey to stir into a cup of tea.

She set the spoon down, and I took one step, closing the distance between us. "You shouldn't do that," I murmured, my voice coming out low and gravelly.

"Do what?"

"Lick the spoon."

Her puzzled eyes met mine. "What's the problem with that?"

"I want to kiss you," I practically growled.

Chapter Five

SASHA

I stared up at Noah, my mouth falling open. "Huh?"

His eyes narrowed as he took a step closer. "I. Want. To. Kiss. You."

Each word out of his mouth came out slowly and deliberately. I heard the words and technically knew the meaning, but my mind just couldn't comprehend them. I'd been a single mom busy raising my daughter for fifteen years, those years encompassing the entirety of my adulthood and the last years of my adolescence. Feeling sexy and the object of anyone's desire was practically a foreign concept to me at this point.

"You do?" I finally squeaked.

"Didn't I just say it twice?" He was starting to look almost annoyed.

"Oh."

"Oh?" he countered. "All you have to do is tell me to back the fuck off. No need to be coy about it."

I rested a hand on my hip. "I'm not being coy. I'm just a little rusty. I can't believe you want to kiss me."

"It's not smart," he said, almost as if to himself.

"What's not smart about it?" I pressed, now almost offended about something I'd thought wasn't possible seconds ago.

"You're Thea's friend."

"And I'm an adult," I sputtered. "For God's sake, I have a fifteen-year-old daughter. Speaking of being coy, just be honest. I know the whole single mom thing is a huge turn-off."

Noah erased the distance between us in a hot second, and I found myself with my hips pressing against the counter and his arms caging me in on either side. "I'm not being coy. I'm never coy. This has nothing to do with you being a single mom. I'm just trying to be sensible, and you're not making it easy," he muttered, his eyes flashing and his voice taut.

A thrill chased through me at his words. Well, that and the fact I could feel his muscled thighs pressing against mine. He carried a subtle, masculine scent, woodsy with a hint of the ocean and snow.

"I've spent my entire adult life being sensible." I heard myself saying, almost startled at my boldness. "What if I don't want to be sensible?"

Noah's nostrils flared, and he took in a sharp breath. "Sasha," he warned.

Determined not to get dismissed, I leaned up, sliding my hand around the back of his neck, and brought my lips to his. The moment we made contact, it felt as if an actual sizzle of electricity linked us. My lips almost burned from the heat of it.

Noah stilled for two electrifying beats of my heart. Then he groaned and angled his head to the side. One of his hands pressed between my shoulder blades, sliding up as his fingers tangled in my hair. He took control of our kiss in a searing second. His tongue slid across the seam of my lips, and I opened, letting out a moan at the feel of his tongue sweeping in and gliding against mine.

I didn't know how long it lasted because I lost track of everything, including time, but our kiss went *absolutely* wild. I arched against him, savoring the feel of his swollen arousal pressing at the apex of my thighs. Our kiss almost felt like a fight. I was fighting to unleash a part of me that had lain dormant for years. Meanwhile, Noah's tongue dueled with mine, his lips sensual and commanding.

Eventually, he drew back, and I felt myself following him, but he held my head still where his palm lightly gripped the nape of my neck. His forehead fell to mine as he pressed a kiss to one corner of my mouth and then the other. "Sasha," he whispered gruffly, "slow down."

"I don't want to," I said, almost pleadingly.

He held me close. The sound of our ragged breathing filled my ears as my heartbeat kicked hard and fast inside my chest. Eventually, a shuffling sound by the kitchen door nudged into my awareness. My thoughts were muddled until I heard Matilda's distinct bark.

"I need to let Matilda in," I murmured into Noah's chest. And what a chest it was, all muscled and strong. I wanted to slide my hands under his T-shirt and map the planes of his body.

Noah stepped back, his eyes searching mine. I suddenly felt uncertain and abashed.

Turning, I crossed quickly to the kitchen door, letting Matilda in. She greeted me with thumps of her tail against my calves before hurrying over to do the same with Noah. Her presence snapped some cold reality through that crazy moment, and I busied myself tidying the kitchen and putting away the things Noah had gotten at the store. He helped for a few minutes, but then his phone rang, and he stepped out of the kitchen.

I crossed over to fill the new tea kettle with water. After I set it on the stove and turned on the burner, I leaned my hips against the counter and curled my hands over the edge. I needed the cold surface of the counter to anchor me. Lifting my head, I stared out through the windows. The snow-covered lawn glittered under the late afternoon sun, and I wondered just how ridiculous Noah thought I was.

But then, I recalled the feel of his lips on mine and the heat of his arousal. His body told me the truth no matter how many doubts crowded my thoughts. Maybe, just maybe, I should take this accidental week with him and have a fling. I trusted Noah, and I knew he wouldn't hurt me. I was far too sensible to let my heart get involved. Maybe, just maybe, this was perfect.

Chapter Six

NOAH

"Got it," I said into the phone. "I'll take care of it when I'm back in the office next week."

"You're not gonna cave and come back early?" my older brother, Dallas, teased.

"No," I said, fighting not to sigh.

"Good," Dallas replied firmly. "You need a break. I only called because you asked me to."

"I did. And thanks to you, I think I might actually be able to take this break."

Dallas chuckled. "Sounds like a plan. Now, I'm not calling you again. I'll see you at Christmas."

The line went dead in my ear, and I lowered my phone, sliding it back into my pocket. I'd followed my older brother into the FBI. Last year, we started working together on a case. I loved working with Dallas because I trusted him implicitly. He'd called to let me know they'd finally made an arrest on a complicated financial fraud case. That was my expertise, which was kind of weird because my father was in jail for pulling off a massive fraud. Well, only temporarily pulling it off.

With a mental shake, I crossed the living room to look out the windows. The evergreen trees flanking the backyard were dusted with snow. Whitecaps ruffled the surface of the ocean in the distance. A gust of wind blew a little swirl of snow off a tree, and the feathers of a blue jay were bright as the bird flew past the windows.

I thought about Sasha and that crazy-hot kiss. Fuck me. I knew it wasn't smart to desire her. It definitely wasn't wise to kiss her. Kissing her only made me want her even more. She kissed with abandon, and she felt so perfect—soft and warm with her curves pressing against me.

I decided, for the moment, to just see what happened. Maybe it was insane, but I wasn't so sure I could keep my hands off delectable Sasha for a full week.

"You're going where?" I asked, glancing up from where I was sitting on the couch in the living room. Although I'd managed to avoid further phone calls from work, I'd been unable to resist pulling out my laptop and checking my email.

"Out to dinner," Sasha replied.

When my eyes met hers, my body instantly tightened. She was wearing a fitted pair of jeans with leather boots that hugged her calves. She wore a silky plum-colored blouse over a camisole, and my eyes landed on the stretch of cotton across her breasts. She had lip gloss on, and I wanted to throw my laptop on the floor, stand, cross to her, and kiss it all off. I swallowed.

"I'll come with you."

Sasha's eyes narrowed, her gaze considering as she looked at me from across the room. I felt as if I were being measured and sized up in her mind. "You've been avoiding me for the past twenty-four hours. Maybe we should stick with that. Apparently, kissing me totally freaked you out."

I closed my laptop and set it on the coffee table before standing. "Kissing you did not freak me out," I said flatly. The rapid thud of my heartbeat in my chest echoed with each word. "I'd like to go to dinner with you." I crossed the room, stopping where she stood in the archway that led into the hallway.

"I wasn't aware I invited you to go with me." Her tone was sharp, but there was a rasp to it, and I didn't miss the way her cheeks pinkened.

"Fine, let me correct that. Would you mind if I went to dinner with you?" I tried to keep my tone crisp, but it came out slightly rough, like the serrated edge of my desire.

Sasha lifted her shoulder in a slight shrug with a saucy lift of her chin. "Fine. I hadn't decided where to go yet. Do you have a preference?"

"How about Emile's? We haven't been there yet."

"Fine. We've only been here so long."

"I wasn't saying that as a complaint," I returned. "Just that I haven't been there in years, and since you haven't been to Haven's Bay in a while, I figured you hadn't either."

"I haven't. Shall we go then?"

"Sure. Let me just grab my jacket."

The heels of Sasha's boots echoed briskly on the floor ahead of me. My eyes tracked the swing of her hips. I'd been lying when I told her kissing her hadn't freaked me out. It had most definitely unsettled me. Just not the way she thought.

Sasha snagged her fluffy down jacket hanging on the coat rack in the corner of the foyer. My jacket was hanging on the end of the banister, and I grabbed it.

"Oh wait, I need to let Matilda out before we go," she said as soon as Matilda came trotting down the stairs. She'd taken to napping upstairs in the sunshine that came through the window and landed on a circular rug at the end of the hall.

It was early evening, and the sun was setting, but it was still probably warm in that spot.

"I'll start my car while you take her out."

Sasha nodded, following me with Matilda right behind us. My car was warm a few minutes later, and Sasha was quiet as I drove into Haven's Bay. The holiday lights glittered under the evening twilight, casting the small downtown area in a charming twinkling glow.

"Wow," Sasha said in a low voice. "I forgot how beautiful the town is over the holidays."

I glanced sideways when I came to a stop at the stoplight. She was looking out the window, and I wanted to reach over and turn her chin toward mine for a kiss. But she was still annoyed with me, so now wasn't the moment for that.

I turned onto Main Street, passing by Haven's Bay Grocery. Holiday lights were strung on the rooftops of the stores and homes in downtown proper. The decorative lampposts had wreaths mounted on them, lining the street with holiday cheer. Another moment later, the sign for Emile's came into view. I slowed and turned into the parking lot, not surprised to see it filled with cars.

As we walked across the parking lot with the sound of our footsteps crunching on the gravel, I commented, "We might have to wait at the bar for a table."

Sasha's eyes slid sideways, her lips kicking up at one corner. Lust bolted through me. "I've never even gotten to sit at the bar here. That's big stuff."

Her reply caught me off guard, and I barked out a laugh as I held the door open for her. "I guess not, seeing as you moved away from town when you were sixteen."

I turned out to be correct. When we stepped inside, every table was full. Even the bar was full, although I spied one barstool and quickly guided Sasha to it. Without thinking, I rested my hand on her lower back, coaxing her forward as we threaded our way through the tables.

I saw people turning as we passed by with some waving or calling out quick greetings. I hadn't been back home too often, but I did know some locals. I honestly didn't know who might recognize Sasha.

"Right here," I murmured, leaning down to speak into her ear.

She slipped her hips onto the barstool, and I leaned my elbows on the bar beside her. She spun around, her eyes arcing about the room. "Wow, it looks pretty much the same."

The restaurant was in a renovated cape-style home with the walls knocked down and supporting beams refinished to create open space. Tables were scattered in the center with a coffee bar on one side, a liquor bar on the other, and a deli counter and kitchen in the back. The place functioned as a coffee shop and deli in the morning into the afternoon. In the evenings, the coffee bar shut down, and alcohol flowed with the food. They served standard pub fare with the seafood twist of mid-coast Maine. In addition to burgers and sandwiches, they had fresh lobster rolls, fish and chips, crab cakes, and the like.

The restaurant was pretty basic as far as

décor went. Over in one corner, there was a pool table. The bar had a glossy wooden surface, and the bartender, Rick, caught my eye, grinning when he recognized me.

"Well, hey there, Noah. Long time." His eyes landed curiously on Sasha. "Do I know you?" he asked as he set two napkins on the bar in front of us.

"Maybe," Sasha replied with a saucy grin. "I'm Sasha Hilts. I grew up here, but I moved away in high school."

Rick nodded slowly, his brows hitching up. "Ah, I remember you. How're things?"

"Pretty good."

"What can I get you two?"

"I'm driving, so I'll just take a water. You?" I glanced at Sasha, not missing Rick's lingering gaze on her. A bolt of possessiveness jolted me.

"What kind of margaritas do you have?" she asked.

"Strawberry and regular."

"I'll take a strawberry one."

"You two waiting for a table?" Rick asked as he quickly filled a glass with ice and water and handed it to me before making Sasha's margarita.

I nodded. "We'd like to sit down to eat."

"Got it." He glanced over just as a server

slipped through the swinging doors into the kitchen in the back. He handed Sasha her drink. "I'll put that on your check for after you eat," he said as he turned away to serve another customer. "Great to see you both."

Minutes later, I decided coming out with Sasha was a bad idea. The guy on the other side of her was flirting with her, and she was flirting back. Grinding my teeth, I was feeling fucking insane. Jealousy wasn't something I had any experience with. Sasha seemed uniquely able to bring a sense of possessiveness out in me. Hell, I wanted to punch the fucking guy and Rick too. Because he kept casting her appreciative looks.

When the server let us know a table was open, Sasha slid her empty margarita glass over toward Rick. "That was delicious. Thank you." Turning to me, she added, "Be right there. I'm going to stop in the ladies' room."

As she walked away, Rick asked me, "You two a couple?"

Because I wasn't thinking rationally, I lied, "Yes."

He chuckled. "Better hold on tight."

Sasha met me at the table minutes later, sitting down with a smile. "You know, I wouldn't trade being a single mom, but it's kind of nice to have a break. Nobody here knows how unglamorous my life is. It's like actually being single instead of being a single mom."

I stared at her across the table and almost growled. "Really?" I managed tightly.

"Why so grumpy?" she asked. She pulled the laminated menu tucked between the salt and pepper from the center of the table and began scanning it.

"I'm not grumpy," I muttered in return.

Her gorgeous green eyes lifted to mine, searching my face. "If you say so."

A minute later, she tucked the menu back between the salt and pepper. "I'm getting a lobster roll. I haven't had one in a while."

"When we're back in Boston, I'll take you to my favorite place for lobster rolls at the docks."

"We?"

"Yes. We both live in Boston. No reason we can't get together there."

She stared back at me, and I didn't know how to read what I saw flickering in her eyes. We had dinner, and it was delicious. My manners kicked in, and I learned more about her life at work. By the time we left, my body was twisted tight for her. Sitting across the table and watching her eat was its own form of torture, made worse by my irrational possessiveness. Every man who looked her way annoyed me. I supposed the worst part was I felt like I'd put myself in the situation.

As we crossed the parking lot toward my car after dinner, Sasha smiled in my direction. "Thanks for going with me. It's nice just to get out."

"Great to see you, Sasha," a voice called. She turned back, waving at the guy who spoke.

"Nice to see you too, Aaron!" she called in return.

I didn't even know Aaron, but they'd had a few classes together in high school. I rounded the car to open the door for her, trying to shackle my urge to kiss her.

But then, she looked up at me. "Remind me why you're so grumpy."

I answered her by leaning down, sliding my hand around the back of her neck, and fitting my mouth over hers. I didn't know what the hell I was doing, but I was done trying to ignore the flames that licked through my body every time she was in my proximity. Hell, I'd fallen asleep last night thinking about her, and she was all the way upstairs.

Sasha made a little sound at the back of

her throat, and her mouth opened, her tongue darting out to slide sensually against mine. With a sigh, she arched into me.

The next thing I knew, I pressed her against my car and kissed her roughly, pouring days of pent-up desire into our kiss. A car door slammed somewhere in the vicinity, puncturing the haze of need clouding my thoughts. I forced myself to lift my head, but it was no easy feat.

Her eyes were dark, and her lips puffy as she stared up at me. "What was that about?"

Fuck me. Even the sound of her voice revved the need driving me.

Chapter Seven

SASHA

"A kiss," Noah answered, his voice gruff and husked with an edge.

A shiver raced over the surface of my skin, goosebumps following in its wake and my nipples tightening to an ache. I was acutely aware of the slick need between my thighs. I shifted restlessly on my feet in a futile effort to relieve the pressure building there.

"I thought that wasn't smart," I said, my voice coming out all breathy.

I felt so foolish around Noah. Maybe I'd been a scandal in high school, but I was anything but since then. I knew he was far more experienced than me, most certainly with having casual fun.

"Maybe I don't care if it's smart or not."

He was plastered against me. I felt the hot, hard press of his arousal in the cradle of my hips and wished we were already home. It was enough that I'd already decided I wanted to act on my desire, but I didn't feel crazy enough to do something about it right here. A gust of wind blew through the parking lot, and I shivered slightly.

He stepped back, and I heard the door latch click when he reached around me. "Let's go home."

A few minutes later, I learned that the small space in a car could feel incredibly crowded. The air felt heavy, almost like a charge about to go off.

I was hot all over with my skin prickly. Need was racing through my body in a loop, and I needed a way to discharge the intense, unfamiliar feeling. I had vague memories of that old high school boyfriend who got me pregnant. When you were young, sex was kind of hit or miss. It wasn't great, but I did remember the excitement before, feeling like maybe something good would happen. The few sexual encounters I'd had since then— dating relationships that went nowhere—had left a lot to be desired.

My endless to-do list was always hovering

in the back of my thoughts. I just couldn't relax enough to enjoy sex. Noah had this strange effect on me, leaving me more turned on than I'd ever been. And I knew him. I knew him well even though I hadn't seen him in years. Maybe it was my younger self who thought he was so handsome and unattainable. Maybe it would turn out to be a disappointment, but I was going to grab this chance.

Because this week would end, and I would return to my life. The ticker of my to-do list would click on like a clock in the background of my life. Every minute counted.

This didn't have to be anything but a suspended week in my life. Even if it was only one night. I didn't care. I wanted it too much to let anything else get in the way.

"Just one night," I whispered, my words landing like sparks on dry kindling.

"One night won't be enough," Noah said flatly, pouring fuel on that kindling.

"How do you know?" My eyes whipped to his as he rolled to a stop in the driveway in front of the house.

He pressed a button, and the engine went quiet. "I just know."

Staring at him in the glimmer of light cast

from the porch light, I felt my mouth go dry and my belly spin. As if I were falling from a great height and didn't know how to slow my fall. Despite, or perhaps because of my internal turmoil, my need felt as if it were ramping up inside, suffusing me and spinning through my veins.

"Oh," I finally said.

A moment later, Noah was walking beside me as we crested the top stair on the porch. I was reaching for the doorknob when Noah caught my free hand. Glancing over, I lifted my brows in question.

"If you don't want this, all you have to do is say so."

His gaze searched mine, and my heart kicked out a wild rhythm. "I do, though," I finally said.

A whining sounded from the other side of the door. My cheeks got hot. "First, I have to let Matilda out."

Noah's chuckle sent heat racing through me.

"Of course." He opened the door, and Matilda dashed out, circling us excitedly in greeting before leaping off the stairs and running to the side of the snow-covered lawn she'd identified as her preferred bathroom area.

Noah waited with me on the porch, and we watched together as she ran through the snow, yipping and snapping at the snow that flew up around her. A few minutes later, I watched as Noah tucked crumpled paper under the logs he'd just placed in the fireplace before tossing the match in. In another moment, the flames were crackling to life.

After we came in, Matilda had happily taken the chew toy Noah tossed her way and settled on her bed in the corner of the living room, focused on the task at hand. Meanwhile, I was a bundle of nerves. Anxiety was tangling up inside my desire, and I didn't like the feeling. I felt a little rusty when it came to sex. My bold proclamation earlier was now feeling ridiculous.

I lifted my wineglass off the coffee table and took a big gulp. The single margarita I'd had at the bar hadn't done anything to soothe my rattled nerves. But then, I didn't want any of my senses muddled. Perhaps I was nervous, but I wasn't about to back down.

Noah turned toward me. His eyes landed on mine immediately. It felt as if sparks were lighting the air between us, snapping and crackling from the taut tension.

I wanted to look away, but I didn't. I stared right back, lifting my chin slightly.

"How come I never noticed you before?" he mused, almost as if to himself.

"Because you were four years ahead of me in school. Way out of my league," I said with a little laugh. "There's also the fact we haven't seen each other in years."

"Is that it then?" he murmured as he crossed the room.

My pulse kicked up a notch. "I don't know," I whispered. "Maybe."

He took another stride and then sat on the couch beside me. "This couch wasn't here before," I said incongruously.

It was a large U-shaped sectional, a perfect size for the expansive room and situated facing the fireplace. With plenty of cushions, it was very comfortable. I didn't even feel bad about Noah sleeping down here.

"No, we didn't have this before. We just got it last year." His arm stretched across my shoulders, and we fell quiet. Desire curled around us like wisps of smoke. While almost nothing was happening, my breath felt short and my pulse skittered out of control.

Noah's fingers began tracing along my collarbone, where his hand rested on the edge of my shoulder. All of my awareness narrowed to that strip of skin under his fingertips.

Who knew my collarbone was an erogenous zone? I certainly didn't.

Heat radiated like licks of fire from that one point, and I almost moaned when his thumb dragged in a lazy stroke along the base of my throat. This was seduction by increments, and I didn't know if I could take it.

Restless, I turned to him. "Kiss me," I whispered in a raspy command.

"As you wish." He held my gaze when his lips brushed over mine, and it felt as if lightning sizzled through me, every nerve set alight.

And then, we tumbled into kiss upon kiss upon kiss. It was all sensation—bold strokes of his tongue, lazy nibbles on my bottom lip, hot kisses dropped at the corners of my mouth, and then his lips sliding over mine again and his tongue claiming my mouth.

I was lost, spinning in a riptide of need and fierce desire. I distantly heard little sounds coming from my throat, a broken moan, a ragged whimper. Somehow, I found myself straddling him on the couch. I felt the hard press of his arousal just under my core, and I wanted him inside me. Now.

"Noah," I gasped, "I need…"

I was lost in another devouring kiss as he cupped my breasts with his palms, his thumbs brushing back and forth across the tight peaks of my nipples. I tried again. "I need..."

He dipped his head, his mouth closing on my nipple through my shirt. With a gasp, my fingers speared his hair. My hips were rocking restlessly, and I felt as if I were already standing on the precipice of a cataclysmic release, which I knew would shake me to my core.

Then he lifted his head, his lips stringing kisses along my sensitive collarbone before he nipped lightly at my ear. I shivered all over, restless and needy in his lap. "Noah, I need..."

Apparently, I was a broken record.

He lifted his head, and I felt his palm slide up to cup my cheek. "Look at me, Sasha."

His gravelly command had my eyes dragging open with an effort. His gaze was hot and deliciously commanding. "We're not rushing. I'm in charge."

My mouth dropped open. "What if I want to be in charge?" I retorted.

He hummed. "Next time. Maybe."

I was about to argue the point, but that was kind of difficult when he planted another one of his masterful kisses on me. I wondered if it was possible to climax just from a kiss. Well, a kiss and the pressure of his arousal against my clit.

I was feeling greedy and needy, and I wanted more. I broke free from our kiss, panting before I gasped, "Take your shirt off."

His eyes held mine in the flickering firelight. He looked way too in control. "We'll get to that."

I let out an annoyed sigh, rocking restlessly over his arousal again and protesting, "You know you want to."

"Oh, I do. Just as I didn't fuck you against my car in the parking lot, I'm not going to rush this. We can rush another time."

He distracted me by dragging his tongue in a slow lick along the side of my neck, then sliding his palms under my shirt and deftly undoing my bra. The feel of his palms, warm on my bare skin, elicited a ragged moan.

Restless though I was, Noah kept me entirely occupied. He teased my nipples, peeled off my blouse, and somewhere along the way, I tossed off my camisole and bra. He blessedly took off his shirt when I asked again. Begging was a better description of what I did.

He felt decadent, strong and muscled, just

as I'd imagined but even better. He had a dusting of hair on his chest that narrowed down over his abdomen. My palms followed the trail, and when I started to unbutton his fly, he took charge yet again. Spinning us around, he stretched me out on the sofa.

I wasn't sure how, but with a little assistance from him, I got my boots off, and he peeled my jeans down. When I moved to hook my thumbs over the elastic band of my panties, he stilled my hands. "Not yet."

"You still have your jeans on," I protested.

Once again, any argument with his methods was lost in a storm of sensation. His palms slid up my calves, pressing my knees apart as he dusted kisses over my belly. His touch was firm but light. He dropped kisses on the insanely sensitive skin on the inside of my thighs, and I was rolling my hips restlessly, desperate for release. I was wet, drenched with my own arousal. I could feel the dampness between my thighs when he dragged his fingers over the silk, teasing just over my swollen clit.

I thought I might die from need before he finally, *finally*, dragged my panties off and teased his fingers through my swollen sex. He sank one finger and then another in my channel, and I convulsed instantly, coming in a noisy rush.

"Oh my," he said.

I lifted my head. "You were taking too long," I explained with a sheepish shrug.

"I'd say I was taking it at exactly the right pace," he murmured. His fingers were still in me, and he drew them out, sinking them in again, the stroke sending pleasure in scattered aftershocks throughout my body.

Before I could think, his mouth was on me. It was all a blur as he teased me expertly to another climax. The light suction on my clit sent me to a shuddering clench that I could hardly stand, but the pressure broke, and I came in ragged breaths.

I was barely aware of him moving away until I felt the cushions give under my knees and I dragged my eyes open. He'd finally taken his jeans off, and I swallowed when I saw his arousal. His cock was long and thick, curving up against his belly. He already had a condom on, and I didn't even know when that happened.

"Are you sure about this?" he asked

"Don't you dare stop now," I ordered.

I savored the feel of his weight coming over me. Everywhere his body touched mine was pure pleasure. He was all hardness to my soft curves. He rested his weight on his elbows on either side of my shoulders. His gaze locked on mine. I could feel the press of his thick crown at my entrance and arched toward him. Because I was that needy. I already wanted more.

Once again, he asked, "Are you sure?"

Curling my legs around his hips, I whispered, "Yes."

He nudged into me, easing in at first. It was a slow glide, and then he surged inside me, seating himself deeply as he let out a low moan.

Chapter Eight

NOAH

My forehead fell to Sasha's, and I couldn't hold back the rough groan that escaped. Her channel pulsed around me with her satiny, clenching heat. She was snug. It felt so good to be buried inside her that my voice was slurred when I spoke.

"Oh God, you feel so good."

Her hips nudged against mine. "Noah, I need—"

I'd been trying to keep the grip on my control, but it was slipping. With her soft body pressed against me and her legs embracing me, I could hardly think.

"Hang on, sweetheart."

Drawing back, I closed my eyes as I filled her again. Her hips bucked against me, like spurs on the flanks of my need. My need was already a racehorse wildly out of control, and I couldn't hold back any longer. I pumped into her in long, deep strokes, savoring every sound she made, the feel of her damp dewy skin pressed against mine, and determined to make sure she came once more before I did. I wanted to see her fly apart on my cock.

"Sasha," I murmured, "look at me, sweetheart."

Her eyes opened in the dim light from the fire, her hips rising to meet my next thrust. I could feel her pussy already clenching and tightening around me. Reaching between us, I pressed my fingers over her slippery wet clit. Her eyes went wide, and then she bit her lip before she trembled all over and clamped tightly around me.

Then and only then did I let go. With two more strokes, my balls tightened, and it felt as if lightning shot from the base of my spine through the top of my head as I pumped my release into her. It was all over but the shouting. She was still rippling around me when I collapsed against her, rolling swiftly so my weight didn't crush her.

Chapter Nine

SASHA

Noah's hand was warm around mine, and I couldn't help but giggle, almost startled at the sound. But then, everything about tonight had been beyond startling.

Noah seemed to nudge me out of all my usual patterns, including the one where I didn't giggle very much. Being a young single mom didn't allow for much frivolity.

"What's so funny?" he asked, his voice low in the hallway.

I looked down at our bare feet against the worn hardwood floorboards. After I'd been sated beyond all measure downstairs on the couch, we'd mostly gotten dressed, but not entirely. I'd been too keyed up to relax just yet, so we watched a few shows, including the latest episodes of my favorite reality show. Although I knew reality shows were anything but reality these days, they were still a good escape, a confection almost.

Matilda's claws clicked on the floor in front of us with her tail swaying in the air as she turned into the bedroom.

"I don't know," I finally replied. "This is all just…" I lifted my hand as we followed Matilda. "I don't know. Not what I expected, I suppose."

Uncertainty slithered through me as I looked up at him. "Are you sleeping upstairs? Or just escorting me up here?"

"I'm definitely not sleeping downstairs," he said bluntly.

A few hours later, I woke in the darkness at the insistence of my bladder. Noah's arm was curled around my shoulders, and my knee was hooked over one of his thighs. I didn't want to get up, but I wasn't going to sleep comfortably through the night until I did.

Reluctantly slipping away from him, I tip-toed across the dark room to the bathroom adjacent to the bedroom. Closing the door behind me, I took care of business and then flicked on the light above the sink to look in the mirror. My hair was a tousled mess, and my cheeks were still flushed. I looked like a woman who had been thoroughly satisfied.

My belly did a little tumble as I stood there alone in the bathroom with only my reflection for company. I didn't know what to think about any of this. No matter what, I had absolutely no regrets. I didn't even know if anything would happen the rest of this week, and I told myself it didn't matter. For the first time in years, I felt like someone other than a harried mother. Not that I wanted to cast off that part of myself. It was genuinely impossible. Yet there was a freedom in stepping out of that role, even if only for a few hours.

I turned off the light and made my way back into bed. Noah reached for me the moment I slid under the covers, murmuring something unintelligible and then letting out a sigh before curling up behind me and spooning me in his embrace.

The following morning, after showering with Noah, which turned out to be a revelation, the cold air struck my cheeks as I stepped outside, watching as Matilda dashed into the snow. I let her frolic for a few minutes before clipping on her lead and walking her down the long driveway. By the time we returned, I could smell coffee when we made our way down the hallway after I had di-vested myself of my jacket and boots.

Noah smiled over at me from where he stood at the counter. "Coffee's ready."

Somehow, although last night and this morning had both been momentous occa-sions for me, I suddenly felt bashful. The morning after was something I had limited experience with. I hadn't had *no* experience with it, just not very much.

I managed something like a smile as I crossed over to him. "Thanks for making cof-fee." Matilda looked up at us expectantly. "Oh, you need breakfast," I said to her.

"I've got it," Noah offered. "Get your coffee."

"Are you sure?"

"I've watched you feed her. It's not com-plicated. You have a measuring cup and her food in a bin."

I wasn't used to having help with any-thing, not even feeding the dog. Of course, Quinn helped plenty with things like that at home, but no one else did.

"Okay." I turned and started pouring a cup of coffee, thinking I shouldn't be this flustered about any of this.

The sound of Matilda's food falling into her bowl met my ears, followed by her wolfing it down in her usual fashion. With coffee in hand, I crossed over to the windows, looking out over the snow-covered yard.

I felt Noah's presence seconds later. He stopped behind me, dropping his head and pressing a kiss at the base of my neck. Goosebumps chased in the wake of his touch, and I took a shallow breath as butterflies tickled my belly. I needed to be casual about this, but he wasn't making it easy.

Turning, I took a swallow of coffee. The rich, dark flavor slid across my tongue, steadying me as I swallowed. I decided honesty was the only option.

"I don't really do this, so I don't know what to do."

"Do what?" he countered.

I was relieved he had a mug of coffee in his hand and took a sip as he rested his hips on the edge of the windowsill. This house had deep, tall windows, tall enough to stand within the wide and generous windowsills.

His eyes held mine expectantly. "I'm a single mom, Noah. That should explain everything." Pausing, I took another sip of coffee. "I don't know how to do this casual thing," I added, my hand kind of flailing in the air, representing how I felt inside.

He nodded slowly. "Well, it's just you and me until Christmas. That's five days away. I don't see why we can't enjoy our privacy thoroughly."

Okay, *thoroughly* was just a word. Yet it signified how I'd felt last night with the way he took care of me. I flushed from head to toe, heat suffusing me. I knew my cheeks were bright pink as I stared back at him. "Oh."

An absolutely brilliant reply on my part. My cheeks got even hotter.

"I mean, unless you'd like to limit us to last night, or this morning, I should say."

I shook my head slowly.

Chapter Ten

NOAH

"I think we should get a tree."

Sasha stared up at me, her cheeks pink from the cold. She was wearing a knit hat with a little pom-pom on top. She looked adorable and fetching. I'd discovered I had a thing for girls who gave off a wholesome vibe.

Because I'd given up trying to pretend I didn't have it bad for her, my boots crunched on the snow as I closed the distance between us and dipped my head to brush my lips across hers. I hadn't meant for it to happen, but in a fiery second, my tongue glided against hers, and we were about to get hot and heavy right here on Main Street in Haven's Bay.

"Well, hello, Noah and Sasha," a voice said.

I lifted my head to see Sherry Levesque smiling at us. We were standing just beyond the parking area for Bay Bistro. She had a bag looped over her wrist.

Sasha turned away from me quickly. "Hi," she squeaked.

"So nice to see you two again. You're getting a Christmas tree for the house, right?" Sherry pressed.

I wondered just how long she'd been nearby. "Of course," I said quickly.

"You should go to Haven's Trees. They still have some good ones left. Emile and I just went the other day. I always wait until the week before Christmas."

"How come?" Sasha asked.

Sherry leaned forward and, speaking in a conspiratorial tone, replied, "Because they go on sale then."

"Good point." I nodded.

"Well, I need to get back to the restaurant," Sherry said with a bright smile. She patted Sasha on the forearm as she passed by. "So good to have you back in town."

A little while later, we walked through rows of Christmas trees. "Are you sure you want to get a big tree?" Sasha asked.

"Yes. My family will love it. We'll decorate the living room. I'll get a wreath for the front door and then put one of these trees in the bay window."

Sasha seemed amused but went along with it. As Sherry had advised, we did find a good deal on the tree. When we went to pay for it, I also purchased a jug of cider and some hot fudge.

After we climbed in the car, Sasha commented, "Ted sure knows how to make some extra cash during the holidays. I bet everyone gets fudge and cider on their way out." She was referring to Ted, the guy who'd run this Christmas tree farm for as long as I could recall.

"Of course, they do," I replied with a chuckle.

That night, I cocked my head to the side as we surveyed the Christmas tree. "What do you think?" Sasha asked.

"It's perfect."

We didn't have any decorations other than the lights we'd picked up at Haven's Bay Grocery. The tree glittered prettily in the window. Matilda had sniffed at it curiously for a few minutes, but otherwise, she let it be.

Sasha looked up at me, biting her lip.

"What are we going to tell your family?" In addition to my younger sister and brother, Dallas was coming up with his wife and toddler son.

"About what?" I countered even though I knew exactly what she was asking.

Her lips pressed in a line. "Us. I think we should just not say—"

I cut her off because I'd already thought about this. "We're not going to pretend nothing's happening. We both live in Boston, and I want to see you when we go back."

"You do?" she squeaked.

"Yes. Is that a problem?"

Sasha looked very uncertain, a twitch of worry forming between her brows as she chewed on her pretty pink bottom lip. Fuck me, her lips were made for kissing, and I wanted to kiss her. Badly.

She swallowed. "I guess I thought it was just a fling," she said slowly.

Somehow, that annoyed me. "You're not a fling to me. I hope you want to see me when we're back in Boston."

"You know I have a daughter, right? I'm not all that glamorous to date," she deadpanned.

"I'm not either. I work a lot, and it can be

high stress. I want a chance to see where this goes. I'd love to meet Quinn when you're ready."

Chapter Eleven

SASHA

"What?" Thea asked, her eyes wide as she stared at me.

"I know, it's crazy, but I... well, I really like him."

Thea's eyes widened as a smile stretched slowly across her face. "Oh, my God, this is perfect."

"It is?"

She gave me a long look. "Yes. You are an incredible mother, and that absolutely should be your first priority, but you also deserve a little romance. So does Noah."

Later that evening, we opened presents under the Christmas tree and toasted the holiday with yummy hot cider. With the house sparsely furnished and only one bedroom set up, Thea had brought multiple air mattresses and the family members had set up in a few of the other rooms. It all felt cozy and relaxed, which I savored.

Noah's arm rested across my shoulders as we sat in front of the fire and laughed with his family. In a funny way, this was the closest thing to family I'd ever had growing up. And I almost needed to pinch myself to realize Noah really wanted a chance with me.

Chapter Twelve

SASHA

"Quinn?" I knocked lightly on her bedroom door. I was greeted with a long silence. "Quinn?" I prompted.

I heard the shuffle of footsteps before my daughter swung her door open. Her dark hair was in a lopsided ponytail, and her dark eyes blinked at me through her glasses. "What?"

"If you need anything, Melanie is right next door."

The only word I could think of to describe my fifteen-year-old daughter's expression was sullen. She scrubbed her toe back and forth on the hardwood floor. The motion drew my eyes downward, and I idly noticed she was wearing mismatched socks—one bright royal blue with stripes and the other pink with polka dots.

"What would I need?" she asked, pushing her glasses up on her nose. "I'm just going to play some video games online. Matilda is here to keep an eye on me."

I glanced over at Matilda who thumped her tail on Quinn's bed where she was comfortably ensconced. "Honey, I don't know what you might need, but I just wanted to remind you to check with her if you need anything."

Quinn nodded slowly. "Mm-hmm. She's always right next door, Mom. Where are you going for dinner?"

"I'm not sure yet. Why don't you ask Noah when he gets here?"

My daughter didn't actually growl, but I imagined if she wasn't trying so hard to play it cool, she would've. Just then, the doorbell rang. Quinn moved to close her door, and I put my hand on it. "I'd like you to meet Noah. He's an old friend."

"And your new boyfriend," she said, complete with an annoyed sigh.

I pressed my lips together. I wasn't quite ready to call Noah my boyfriend, but I wasn't about to get into that little debate with my daughter.

"Come on," I said with as much gentleness as I could muster in my tone.

With another heavy sigh, Quinn followed me silently down the hallway to the living room. We didn't have a large apartment. We had exactly what I could afford—a small two-bedroom in Boston. It was a common New England setup—an old home renovated into apartments. We shared the second floor with Melanie. She was a good friend and had babysat Quinn when she was younger. Quinn didn't need a babysitter these days, but I liked having someone for her to check in with if needed. Melanie was a godsend.

The small hallway in my place had two bedrooms and a bathroom with laundry. The rest of the apartment was a living room with a small archway into a kitchen.

I opened the door, and the moment I saw Noah standing on the other side, my belly did a quick flip. I abruptly got nervous and fluttery—a feeling I did *not* want to have in front of my daughter.

Noah's shoulder rested against the wall with his hand tucked in his pocket. He looked good enough to eat. Based on what he was wearing, I presumed he had come here straight from work. He wore slacks with leather shoes paired with a navy down jacket over a button-down. He glanced up, smiling the second he saw me. My pulse revved like a little engine in my body. My own lips tugged into a smile instantly, and I felt like a foolish girl.

My flustered state was made worse with Quinn's watchful eyes. "Come in," I said quickly.

Noah stepped through the door, and Matilda circled his legs. He greeted her with a thorough scratch behind her ears before she trotted away. Quinn was hovering several feet back, her arms crossed tightly and the foot with the pink polka dot sock tapping on the rug. Inexplicably, I recalled that she had picked out that rug. She loved that brightly woven rug. She'd decorated most of the apartment. It had been done in bits and pieces when we could afford new things and when she was old enough to have opinions.

It wasn't as if I'd never been on a date before. It's just I'd never been on a date with a man I really liked. I worried that I liked Noah too much. I didn't even really know what to do with him, much less how to incorporate him into my life with Quinn or if he even wanted that.

Gah! There was no instruction manual for dating with kids, much less with teenagers. I thought maybe I could find a self-help book on it. But, even then, every situation was so unique.

Quinn looked at Noah, her lips pressed in a tight line. She lifted her chin as if she were daring him.

"Noah, this is my daughter, Quinn." I gestured back and forth between them. "Quinn, this is Noah. I've known him—" I began

She interrupted me quickly. "I know ... since you were a kid." She cleared her throat. "Nice to meet you."

Noah looked at her quietly, his eyes warm. "Nice to meet you as well."

He held his hand out, and I held my breath. I honestly didn't know if she was going to shake his hand. I *really* didn't want to have to prompt her to be polite.

After several seconds, she uncrossed her arms and shook his hand rather vigorously. She then surprised me by asking, "Where are you going to dinner?"

Noah shrugged easily as she dropped his hand. "I hadn't decided. Do you have any recommendations?"

Quinn liked that. I could tell. While she didn't actually smile, I could see the hint of one glimmering in her eyes. She twisted her lips, tapping her toe. "Mom likes lobster rolls.

She also likes good Italian food. It can't be shitty or cheap."

"What if cheap is still good?" Noah countered, a grin teasing at the corners of his mouth.

Thank God he had enough sense not to try to pull me into this conversation. The minute Quinn thought he was trying to have a private joke with me, her hackles would rise.

Quinn nodded, blinking behind her glasses. "Well, in that case, that's fine."

"Is there something you would like if we brought takeout home for you?" Noah added.

Quinn bit her lip, tapping that pink polka-dotted toe again. "Maybe. It's cold out tonight, so I think Italian. A good calzone. Lobster rolls are better in the summer," Quinn offered.

"True," Noah said with a quick nod. "That's when the lobster is fresh. We'll get Italian. I know a place with excellent calzones. Shall I put your order in my phone, or does your mom know your favorite?"

Quinn actually smiled, although she was still eyeing him skeptically. "She knows. But it's Greek."

"Got it."

Quinn looked at me. "Have fun."

"Text me if you need anything," I called as she began walking away.

"I'll text Melanie," she called over her shoulder.

Noah glanced toward her and back to me, a subtle smile teasing his lips again. I reached for my coat, sliding my arms into it just as her door closed.

"Well, she didn't slam it," I offered as I glanced up at him.

Stepping closer, he dipped his head and brushed his lips across mine. I thought he meant for it to be a brief kiss, but I was wrong. He brought me flush against his body, his palm sliding up my back to cup my nape as he dropped kisses on each corner of my mouth before fitting his mouth over mine and sliding his tongue between the seam of my lips. I was breathless by the time he drew back.

"Noah!" I whispered.

"I missed you," he said, entirely unrepentant. "Her door is closed, and she can't see us."

I shook my head as I zipped up my jacket and then reached for my purse. Noah curled his hand around mine when we stepped through the door.

"Who is Melanie?" he asked as we walked

down the stairs to the main entrance on the first floor.

"My neighbor. She's in the apartment across the hallway upstairs. She's lived there since we moved in and owns the building. She used to babysit when Quinn was younger, and now she's there if I ever need her in a pinch. Quinn doesn't really need a babysitter when I'm gone for a few hours, but I like having someone nearby."

Noah held the door open, waiting as I walked through. The cold winter air of January in Boston struck my cheeks when I stepped outside.

"That's nice." He caught my hand as the door swung shut behind us.

This was the first time we'd seen each other since last week in Haven's Bay. Although it had been only four days since we got back, our time there felt like a distant memory. It was so separate from my day-to-day life. Even if my vacation hadn't included hot nights with Noah, it was nothing like my regular life.

I'd missed him acutely, which was unsettling for me. I'd discovered that he was a reliable caller and texter. He had called me every single day since we'd gotten back from Boston. He tried to persuade me to go to dinner sooner, but I told him I wanted to give Quinn a few days to adjust to the idea. She'd scoffed at me when I told her that.

Moments later, the holiday lights glittered as we drove through Boston. "Where are you taking me?"

"Obviously, an Italian place with great calzones," he teased. "I know a good one. It's actually right in downtown Boston. We don't have to worry about parking."

Downtown parking in Boston was a forever challenge. "No?"

"We'll use the parking lot for my work. That's one handy perk of having to drive downtown for work every day."

"I don't even know where you live in Boston," I commented. "How long is your commute?"

"I actually don't live that far from you. About five minutes by car and maybe a fifteen-minute walk."

"Really?"

He nodded and turned onto the street that led to downtown Boston. "We didn't really discuss our Boston lives much last week. It's a good neighborhood, but not right downtown and sort of affordable."

I laughed. "Absolutely. I suppose it is logical. I lucked into my place. Melanie knows my boss and gave me a good price. I don't know if I could have afforded it without that connection."

Noah nodded before adding, "Quinn looks a lot like you. She seems like a nice kid."

"I'm glad she was polite tonight. She's not accustomed to me dating anyone."

"No?"

"We already had this conversation. I hardly ever date. I've dated so little she doesn't even know I've dated. I think she's a little worried because I already know you, so she thinks it's going to be a thing."

"A thing?"

"Her description, not mine," I said dryly.

"What is a thing?"

"According to her, it's a relationship. She teased me and then cried, so..." My words trailed off, and a sigh slipped out.

I was startled when I felt Noah's hand curl around mine, pulling it from my lap. His thumb brushed along the side of my wrist. "She's fifteen, and she's had you all to herself. It'll be an adjustment for her."

I glanced at his profile, taking in the strong, clean lines. My belly flipped again, and my heart clanged like a bell in my chest. "I know. Is this a good idea?"

"Having dinner?" His eyes slipped briefly to mine and then ahead again as he came to a stop at a stoplight.

"Yes, this whole thing." I waved a hand vaguely in the air. I was a nervous wreck, and I hated it.

"Sasha, I think it is. You're not just a fling to me. I know we have to take it one step at a time with Quinn. She's important to me, even if I just met her."

Chapter Thirteen

NOAH

Sasha traced her fingertip in a little circle on the table. Her focus dipped down, moving her fingertip more deliberately along the circular edge of a plate.

I reached across the table, catching her hand with mine. "What are you worried about?"

Her eyes whipped up to mine. "Everything. I know you're not purposely being cavalier, but introducing anyone to my daughter is filled with landmines. I don't want to hurt her. I don't want her to think we're rushing into things, but then I also don't want her to think this is just something casual for me."

I took it as a win that Sasha didn't yank her hand away. I brushed my thumb over the back of her palm before turning her hand over and lifting it to press a kiss in the center. When I looked back toward her, pink was cresting on her cheeks. I was grateful for the subtle clue that perhaps I affected her even a little bit as much as she affected me.

Maybe I'd lost my mind, but I wanted Sasha, and I was already committed. My heart was hers. By nature, I was skeptical. If anyone had told me I would go up to Haven's Bay for a week and fall in love, I would've scoffed.

But I knew Sasha, even if it had been years since we'd seen each other. The kind of passion we shared was like catching lightning in a bottle. We couldn't capture it. All you could do was hope, and maybe you'd get a taste of it. For us, I knew it wasn't going to be fleeting.

The emotions between us ran deep. I knew I couldn't rush her, not just because she was Sasha and perhaps more cynical than me, but because everything she said about Quinn was true. It would be confusing for Quinn if I instantly planted myself in her life. So I would take it slow, even though that wouldn't be easy.

"I understand. I'm not a single parent, but I get that you have to somehow find a balance between not rushing it yet not being too casual. We'll take it slow. I promise." My heart was kicking hard in my chest with every word.

At that moment, a server arrived at our table, his alert gaze bouncing between us. "Shall I give you a few more minutes?" he inquired.

Sasha shook her head, her eyes shifting toward him. "I already know what I want."

After ordering, I made sure to request Quinn's calzone to go for when we were ready to leave.

Sasha interjected, "Noah, she doesn't need a large."

"Calzones make excellent leftovers," I pointed out.

Sasha rolled her eyes and smiled. "She'll appreciate it."

"I missed you," I said as soon as the server was out of earshot.

Her cheeks went pink again, and she took a sip of her water. "It's only been four days."

"I don't care how many days it's been. I still missed you."

Her lips twitched into a smile. "I missed you too," she said under her breath in a rush.

"Good to know. How was work?" I asked,

thinking it would be best to focus on something mundane.

Even if I knew I had fallen for Sasha, I was a realistic man. We'd started this in a place of nostalgia for both of us, and now it was back to real life, back to the grind.

Sasha brightened at that, relaxing back into her chair. "Busy. I'm sure it's the same for you, or perhaps not, but whenever I'm gone, which isn't often, I feel like I'm playing catch-up when I get back. There's a price to pay for taking a vacation."

I nodded. "Always. You've told me that you work as a paralegal for an attorney, but what's the focus of the practice?"

"Mostly family law. That's her passion. She also does some drier things like will preparation and so on. Nothing as eventful as the attorneys you deal with, I'm sure."

I shrugged. "No matter the focus, when it's what you do all day, it can seem repetitive at times."

"What's your job at the FBI like?"

"Sometimes exciting, usually stressful, and occasionally boring. We're always working on cases, but we only have what I call TV events every once in a while."

"TV events?" she prompted.

"Most of our cases are dry. Most people

plead down. Every so often, we get big cases that involve news interviews."

"You and Dallas were a part of the case against your father, weren't you?"

"Only in the beginning. Then we became witnesses. Dallas and I both work in the financial fraud section. We weren't looking to investigate our father, but threads in another investigation brought us to him. As soon as that happened, we both had to be taken off the case."

I was used to telling the story, but Sasha's face pinched. "That sucks."

"It did, but it's okay." My father's story was old news in the family, and I preferred not to dwell on it.

Our server arrived to deliver our appetizers at that moment, so the conversation shifted to lighter topics. Having dinner out wasn't something I did often. My job made it easy to throw myself into work and avoid attachments. Sasha tugged on the ties around my heart. She'd already loosened them and slipped right in.

I set the container holding Quinn's calzone in the back seat. It wasn't that late. As much as my body wanted me to persuade Sasha to come home with me, I knew it wasn't an option tonight because of Quinn. I didn't want to bring her home too late for the very same reason.

"What is a normal weekend night like for Quinn?" I asked once we were driving.

"It varies. Sometimes, she does things with friends, and sometimes, she likes to stay at home and play video games or watch shows. It's a toss-up. She's not as caught up in her phone as some teens, or so I hear, but I definitely think she considers it an extra body part."

I chuckled at that. "Right? A friend of mine at work has teenagers, and he tells me their phones are his only leverage."

Her throaty laughter sent lust sizzling up my spine. "Oh, it's leverage, all right." Her laughter quieted. "Honestly, Quinn's a good kid. I keep waiting for her to be more of a difficult teenager, but she hasn't been that bad. She gets irritable, but she tends to withdraw when she's not in a good mood, so it's not horrible. Her grades are good. Thank goodness for that. She reminds me that as long as she doesn't get pregnant as a teenager like I did, I should just deal with it."

"Ouch. That's harsh. She doesn't realize how easy it is to get pregnant."

Sasha laughed hysterically at that. "I've definitely told her. I don't think she's sexually active yet. If she is, she's not telling me. She's on birth control, though."

This was the first moment when I contemplated what it would mean to get serious with Sasha. Teenagers could be truly terrifying. The idea of worrying about a young teenage girl and what someone might do to break her heart was not something I wanted to consider.

"Having a heart attack over there?" Sasha teased lightly.

I glanced to my side, giving her a sheepish smile. "Maybe a little. I don't like worrying about that for a teenager I care about."

"You just met her tonight, Noah," she chided softly.

I reached for her hand, lacing my fingers through hers and squeezing. "I know you don't believe me, but you matter to me. Maybe I just met Quinn, but I care about her by extension because I care about you."

I was gratified that she gave my hand a squeeze. "I'll believe it. If you had a daughter, I would care."

The rest of the ride home was quiet, and I marveled, yet again, that I slipped into this relationship with Sasha so easily. It was just comfortable with her. Well, when we were naked, comfortable wasn't the word I would use. More like pure fire.

When I stopped in front of the house where her apartment was, I glanced over. "Would you like me to come up, or is that too much?"

Sasha held my gaze for a few beats, and I couldn't resist kissing her. Leaning across the console, I took her mouth. I meant for it to be brief, but touching Sasha was like tossing a match in dry leaves. The fire flashed high and fast.

Her tongue glided against mine. When I heard a little catch in her throat, followed by a moan, another match was thrown in the fire. By the time I drew back, I was gasping for breath, right along with her.

"Jesus, Sasha." I leaned my head back against the seat, scrambling to get control of my body's response to her.

She giggled, and the sound spun around my heart. "That was your fault. Why don't you come up? You've got the calzone, after all."

I almost pumped my fists in the air. That was how deep into this I already was.

Chapter Fourteen

NOAH

We walked up the stairs together, but Sasha released my hand when we entered the apartment. Quinn lounged on the sectional over to one side with a TV and a low table against the wall. She had her knees curled up, and Matilda was napping on the couch beside her.

As soon as she saw me, Matilda jumped off the couch and hurried over to greet us both. Maybe I was taking a liberty, but I slipped out of my shoes when Sasha did and hung my coat on the coatrack by the door.

Quinn glanced over, her eyes landing on the box that held the calzone before bouncing to her mother and back to me. "Hi," she said simply.

"Hey, sweetie." Sasha crossed over and dropped a kiss onto Quinn's upturned cheek. "Noah got your calzone. If it's anything like the rest of the food we got, I promise it's delicious."

Quinn uncurled her feet from where they were tucked under her knees and stood, crossing over to us.

I handed her the box. "I got you a large. Your mom said you like leftovers."

Quinn narrowed her eyes and offered me a thank-you as I handed the box to her.

She stood still in the living room, looking between Sasha and me. "Can I have some tonight?" Her eyes landed on her mother with her question.

Sasha nodded. "Of course. We even made sure to get it at the end so it should still be warm."

Quinn cast a quick smile. It was so much like Sasha's that my heart swelled. She skipped across the living room through the archway into what I could see was the kitchen.

Sasha mouthed, "Thank you. She'll love it." After a pause, Sasha asked aloud, "What are you watching?"

"That baking show. The one you love."

Quinn was already returning to the living room with half her calzone on a plate.

Sasha cast me a sheepish smile. "I love *The Great British Baking Show*."

"Do you want to watch some with us?" Quinn asked, surprising me.

When I glanced in her direction, I didn't miss the dare in her eyes. Honestly, any excuse to spend time with Sasha worked for me. "I'd love to."

That was how I found myself on the couch with Sasha between Quinn and me. Sasha even let me hold her hand. The only downside was I wanted to do a lot more than that. Who knew teenagers made the best chaperones in the world? With Quinn's perceptive gaze occasionally glancing our way, I didn't dare do anything more than hold Sasha's hand.

At one point, Sasha went to the bathroom. As soon as the sound of the door clicking shut reached us, Quinn pinned me with her eyes. "Don't you dare hurt my mom," she said fiercely.

I was used to feeling like I could go with the flow of any conversation. I was also used to feeling like I had my shit together. Hell, I was an FBI agent and handled high-end financial fraud. Questioning those suspects was challenging because they usually had a lot of money and were accustomed to getting their way or buying their way out of tight spots.

But Sasha's protective teenage daughter had me feeling like I didn't know what to say. I cleared my throat. "I'm not planning on hurting your mother." Stating the obvious was always a good place to start.

"Of course, you're not planning on it. Even assholes don't plan on it."

My heart ached a little for this girl who clearly loved her mother and wanted to make sure no one hurt her.

"I know you just met me, but I promise your mom means a lot to me, and I have no intention of hurting her."

Quinn's lips pressed together and twisted to the side as she blinked at me. "It's just she's never introduced me to any-one. She's trying to play it cool, but she's *so* not cool."

I bit the insides of my cheeks to keep from laughing because Quinn was dead seri-ous. I nodded slowly. "I understand your point. I don't think your mom would've in-troduced me if—"

I cut myself off. I didn't know what to say to this girl to convince her that what I wanted was her mother to realize we had a real thing here.

Quinn nodded as if I had somehow done something to satisfy her. "Good, you don't know what to say either."

"What the hell does that mean?" I countered, abruptly wondering if hell counted as a curse word and if I could say it in front of a fifteen-year-old, specifically Sasha's daughter.

As if she freaking read my mind, Quinn offered, "Hell is a place, not a swear word. Mom swears in front of me if you were wondering. She tries not to, but she slips up." At my chuckle, she continued, "My point was, you're not trying to be slick. If you were, then as soon as you left, I would tell her not to go to dinner with you again. But you're not slick, and you're not cool. And, apparently, you're stumbling over how to explain how you feel, so that's a good sign."

Sasha happened to return to the living room at this moment, her eyes bouncing between us. "Quinn, what did you say to Noah?"

It was only then I realized my mouth had actually dropped open. Good Lord, her daughter had me gaping like a fish.

Quinn thought the whole thing was hysterical and threw her head back with a laugh. "Nothing," she said when she finished laughing. Sasha sat down beside me again. "I was just asking him his intentions."

Sasha's cheeks went pink. "Quinn! It was a dinner date. You're also not my parent. I'm your mother."

"Yeah, but you don't date." Quinn arched a brow, her eyes glinting with mirth.

Sasha glanced at me. "I am so sorry."

"No need to apologize. It was rather clarifying."

Sasha narrowed her eyes as she looked toward Quinn again. Quinn finally stopped giving me the side-eye and enjoyed her calzone. She even told me that it was really good.

After the show was over, I decided it was best to leave on a high note. I said my goodbye to Quinn, and Sasha walked into the hallway with me. When the latch on the door clicked behind us, I spun her around, pressing her against the wall and dipping my head to breathe in her scent along the side of her neck.

I felt the shiver run through her and couldn't resist dropping a hot kiss just below her ear. That led to another and another before I dragged my tongue along the side of her neck, nipping lightly as she arched into me, letting out a low moan. My cock was swollen and aching. Desperate for more, I lifted my head, claiming her mouth with mine. God, I fucking *loved* kissing her. She made these little sounds in her throat that drove me wild. I could feel her warm, soft curves pressing against my chest.

My hand slipped under the hem of her shirt, coasting over the curve of her belly and cupping a breast. I could feel the tight peak of her nipple and pinched it lightly. She rocked her hips against mine. I slid my other hand down to cup her bottom, pressing her against my arousal. I was throbbing for her. I was on the verge of finding my release in my pants, something I hadn't done since I was a teenage boy. One kiss led to the next, and her palm slid under my shirt, her touch silky and smooth.

I didn't even hear the door behind us open until a voice said, "Excuse me."

My lips broke from Sasha's abruptly as I lifted my head and glanced over my shoulder. I kept Sasha shielded, seeing as I had one hand up her shirt.

An elderly woman was standing in the doorway directly across the hall. She had curly silver hair and wore a hot-pink bathrobe with bunny slippers. She eyed me with unabashed curiosity. "You must be Noah," she announced.

I managed to stealthily get my hand out from under Sasha's clothes. Blessedly, I had already put my jacket on before I walked out the door, so I smoothly adjusted it to obscure my arousal as I turned.

Sasha looked over at the woman I presumed was her neighbor, Melanie. "Hey there. Eavesdropping?" she teased.

Oh, good. Sasha didn't seem too upset at the interruption.

"Of course. Somebody's got to get some around here."

Sasha rolled her eyes. "This is Noah." Looking at me, she added with a sweep of her hand toward the woman, "And this is Melanie."

"Nice to meet you, Noah," she said with a smile.

"Likewise," I offered.

"I'm not a witch, just a nosy old lady. Plus, I keep an eye on things," Melanie offered with a grin.

"Much appreciated," I replied, dipping my chin in acknowledgment.

"You best do right by Sasha," Melanie added.

"Melanie!" Sasha pushed away from the wall. "He's an old friend."

"I'm here, you know. You don't have to talk about me like I'm not."

Melanie ignored me, casting a sharp eye on Sasha. "I have a bone to pick with him, not you."

Good grief. First Quinn, now the neighbor. Sasha had not warned me that she had a gauntlet I had to pass and more than one test on the way to winning her heart.

"I promise I will do right by her," I said, addressing Melanie. "I already told Quinn something along the same lines."

Melanie nodded. Her gaze swept from the top of my head all the way down to my shoes and back up. Nothing about it was sexual, but holy hell, I felt as if she were X-raying me.

She looked toward Sasha. "He's cute. He'll do."

Sasha's cheeks were bright red. "After Quinn and this, he'll probably never come back."

"No chance of that." I laughed because what I wanted to say was for Sasha's ears only.

"He'll be back," Melanie said confidently.

"Nice to meet you." She closed her door, and we could hear the bolt sliding in place.

"Sorry about that," Sasha said with a shake of her head. "I'll walk you down."

We stopped on the landing at the bottom of the stairs. I stepped to her, palming her cheek and looking into her eyes. "You're not going to scare me away, Sasha." I dusted a kiss across her lips.

"What about Quinn and Melanie?" Her eyes searched mine.

"Nope."

I couldn't resist one more kiss, although that didn't help with the state of my cock, which protested mightily as I drew back. I'd have to take matters into my own hands tonight.

"How about I take you and Quinn to dinner tomorrow night?"

Sasha's eyes widened comically. "Are you serious?" she sputtered.

Chapter Fifteen

SASHA

By the time Noah left, on the heels of another breath-stealing kiss, I had to lean against the wall in the foyer downstairs. I needed a minute to gather myself and scramble my wits together. Once I could breathe and my knees weren't threatening to give out, I headed back upstairs.

The second I crested the top stair onto the landing on the second floor, Melanie's door flew open. Her grin was wide. "Noah is totally hot," she announced. Melanie might not be young, but she acted like it sometimes.

I was hot all over. I bit my lip and tried to give a nonchalant shrug. "I won't argue the point on that."

Her eyes took on a gleam as they swept from my head to my toes. "He kissed you again, didn't he?"

I leaned against the railing at the top of the stairs. "You know, you're seventy-five years old," I pointed out, completely side-stepping her question.

"Obvious much?" she countered quickly. "So what? I may not be getting any myself, and frankly, I'm past that stage, but I can certainly enjoy it vicariously."

I sighed. "Yes, he kissed me again."

"Want some tea?"

I could always use a late-night chat in Melanie's comfortable kitchen. I nodded. "As if I'd say no."

I followed her into her apartment, which was basically a mirror of Quinn's and mine. We walked through the archway into her small kitchen. She filled the kettle, setting it on the stove.

We'd been neighbors and friends long enough that I didn't wait for her to tell me to have a seat. That was a given. Just as she had a key to our place and could come over anytime for dinner, or tea, or whatever.

The anxiety that had welled after Noah left started to dissipate. Frankly, I didn't know what to do about this man who turned me on like no other and who was so comfortable because I knew him from before. Yet I didn't know how this would play out.

"What kind of tea?" Melanie asked over her shoulder as she pulled two mugs out of the cabinet by the sink.

"Do you have chamomile? I need something that will help me fall asleep."

"Of course you need something to help you fall asleep. I'm sure you're wide awake. Yes, I have it."

I laughed. A few minutes later, Melanie was sitting across from me, and steam rose from our respective cups of tea.

"So that was Noah," she began.

"Yep." I lifted my teacup to take a sip, but it was too hot. I set it down on the table. "He wants to take Quinn and me to dinner tomorrow. I'm not sure about that."

"What does Quinn think?"

"I'm not sure. He asked me in the hallway. She was polite tonight. He also bribed her with a calzone."

"From where?"

"I forgot what it's called. It's right near that sandwich place we love by the old bank. It really is good."

Melanie's eyes lit up. "Oooh, I've been there. Very good place, but not too trendy."

"Yeah. You've heard of it?"

Melanie smiled. "Of course I have. My John used to take me there. We loved it. You forget, but we lived over in that area when I was in college. It was a long time ago, and I don't drive these days, but I'm sure the same family owns it. Smart man to offer to get Quinn a calzone. I know how much she loves those."

"I know." I took a breath, letting it out before finally taking a sip of my tea. "Do you think I'm crazy?"

Melanie gave me a dry look. "Absolutely not. You went on a date. It's not like you have to worry about this man doing anything horrible. You've known him and his family for years."

I'd told Melanie a little bit about Noah after my week in Haven's Bay with him. "Yeah, but Quinn's not used to me dating."

Melanie tightened her lips and cast me something approaching a glare. "You don't need to be alone forever. If I didn't know better, I'd think you were aiming for that. You're not irresponsible. You haven't been dating and running through men faster than some people do their rosary beads when they pray." I snorted at that. "It's obvious he likes you. And he's a honey, very easy on the eyes."

A "honey" was Melanie's description of a cute guy. She tended to select the men who did repairs on the building based on how cute they were. I doubted the wisdom of that, but she'd never had an issue.

I rolled my eyes. "I'll ask Quinn if she wants to have dinner. If she wants to go, we'll do it."

"It's a good sign he wants to include her this soon. She's the most important person in your life."

"Of course, she is." I took another swallow of my tea. "I wish there was an instruction manual."

"For what?"

"Dating as a single parent."

"Sweetie, dating is fraught whether you're a single parent or not. I'm not going to pretend it's not more difficult when you have a daughter to consider. I think you're a little rusty. Might as well try with someone who obviously thinks you're sexy and wants you."

I rolled my eyes. "Right now, he does. But wait until I have to cancel for one in a long list of reasons. Or wait until Quinn decides she hates him."

"Or wait until it's not as bad as you think," Melanie pointed out.

Chapter Sixteen

SASHA

Quinn blinked at me from where she sat across the table. "Dinner?"

I was unaccountably nervous. It was some combination of not really having any romantic relationships as an adult, *really* liking Noah, and having my daughter look at me as if I were an unwanted bug.

"Yes, dinner with Noah and me."

Quinn looked down, taking a bite of her oatmeal before her lashes swept up, and she pinned me with her skeptical gaze again. "Why is he trying so hard?"

"Sweetie—" I began.

Quinn shook her head as if I didn't understand something. "Mom, he totally has the hots for you. He's just trying to get in your pants through me."

I stuttered on the sip of coffee I had just taken. "Oh, my God. Quinn!"

She gave me a satisfied smirk. "He is."

Putting aside her comment about his motives, I forged ahead. "I've known him since I was a little girl. He's a nice man and would like to get to know you."

Quinn tapped my knee with her socked foot. "It's fine, Mom. I'll go. He doesn't seem like a bad guy."

I did my best to take a deep breath carefully, so Quinn didn't notice when I let out a slow and quiet sigh of relief.

"Where would you like to go?" I asked next.

"Well, Noah was right about that Italian place. It's good. Why doesn't he find a new Thai place we haven't tried?"

"Is this a test that's impossible for him to pass?" I asked skeptically.

Quinn cast me a sly grin. "Maybe, but I won't be too hard on him."

I rolled my eyes. "Okay, then. I'll let him know."

We spun into our usual busy morning routine. Quinn finished her breakfast and jumped in the shower while I got dressed.

After I dropped her off on the way in and parked in the lot for work, I took a moment to send Noah a text.

I thanked the gods daily that Noah didn't expect frequent texts. I didn't have time when I was at work, and neither did he. We'd fallen into the habit of texting each other in the morning. When I opened my phone, his text was waiting.

Noah: *Morning, gorgeous. Tell me what Quinn says about dinner.*

Me: *Morning. Quinn says yes. She has given you the assignment of finding an amazing Thai place we haven't tried yet. Can't wait to see you.*

Just texting him sent my belly into a swoop. I took a breath and slipped my phone into my purse before running into the office.

Chapter Seventeen

NOAH

"You're kidding," I muttered as I lifted my head and looked up at the doorway of my office.

My older brother, Dallas, stood there. He rested his shoulder on the inside of the door-frame, shaking his head. "Definitely not kidding. I want you on this one with me."

"You'd have to fight to keep me off," I replied as I leaned back in my chair, picking up a miniature Slinky I kept on my desk and spinning it on my forefinger.

Dallas stepped into my office, closing the door behind him. He slipped into the chair across from my desk. "I hate this shit."

"Money always leads us in interesting directions."

Dallas and I both worked in the FBI and specialized in financial fraud. Often, our cases started with one thread that unraveled into several. In this particular case, we'd been looking at money laundering through a bank that was leading us to a massive identity theft operation.

"I can't believe Jones would risk this." I was referring to a local Boston politician. Matty Jones had been a fixture in Boston politics for two decades, following his father's footsteps to the Boston City Council. They reigned supreme in terms of business influence around town and liked it that way.

Dirty money was always mucking up politics anywhere in the world, but this little turn was a surprise. The Jones family tended to play it smart and careful.

Dallas shrugged. "I know. Let's see where it takes us." His phone buzzed, and he slipped it out of his pocket. "Hang on, let me take this."

I nodded and glanced back at my computer screen, scrolling through my email.

"Hey, love," he said, quickly lifting the phone to his ear after he swiped his thumb across the screen.

I knew that meant Audrey, his wife, was on the other end. The moment I thought of

Audrey, my mind squirreled to Sasha. Lately, many thought roads led to Sasha, but Audrey brought her to mind because they'd been in school together. I wondered if they stayed in touch.

"On my way," Dallas said as he ended the call.

I grinned when he stood. "You have become very good at leaving work on time," I observed.

Dallas shrugged, casting an easy smile. "I've got a woman I love and a son to go home to. Work doesn't compete."

I chuckled.

"Speaking of," Dallas began, "have you seen Sasha since you've been back to Boston?"

"Just last night. I'm taking her and Quinn to dinner tonight."

A knowing glint entered my brother's eyes. "Do you like her?"

"Definitely." I didn't even bother to hide it. Dallas knew me well.

His gaze sobered. "It's a package deal, you know?"

"With her daughter, you mean?" At his nod, I added, "I know. That's why I'm taking them to dinner tonight. I met her last night. She's a nice girl."

Dallas turned to leave. "If you need someone to vouch for you, I'm your man." He tapped the door in emphasis on his way out.

———

Quinn pushed her glasses up on her nose as she studied the menu. Although she was fully a teenager at fifteen, somehow that gesture made my heart twinge a little. It made her seem younger than her years. She seemed to have assumed the role of Sasha's gatekeeper, casting me a sort of glowering look and asking pointed questions.

After we ordered, the conversation actually went easier than I anticipated. Quinn was polite and delightful with a quirky and blunt sense of humor. She had lots of questions about my job, which was easy enough to talk about. I was an expert at keeping discussions general so as to avoid complications.

When I walked up to the apartment with them afterward, Quinn gave me a cautious look in the living room. "You can stay for a little bit. I'm going to my room."

Sasha rolled her eyes, crossing to her. "Good night, sweetie. Don't forget, we have errands tomorrow."

"How could I?" Quinn drawled as she turned before spinning back and kissing her mother on the cheek. She called, "Thanks for dinner!" just before sprinting to her room.

After her door closed, Sasha looked at me. "Do you want to stay for a little while? You don't have to."

"As if I'd say no," I said bluntly. I shrugged out of my winter jacket, hanging it on the coat rack by the door and slipping off my shoes.

"Do you want something to drink?" Sasha asked from where she stood in the archway that divided the living room and kitchen areas. She looked restless with her fingers twining together.

"Maybe water? I've still got to drive home even though it's not far."

A moment later, she sat on the couch beside me, setting two glasses of water on the coffee table beside it. She sat cross-legged and looked over at me. "Thanks for taking Quinn with us. I hope it wasn't too awkward."

"Not at all." I reached for her hand to discover it was cold. I gave her a little tug, and she scooted closer. Her eyes searched mine. "Quinn's your daughter. It's not awkward to have dinner with her."

Sasha bit her lip. "I'm not used to dating, much less anyone who didn't run because I have a teenage daughter."

"Sasha, I know you, and I know your life. She's a good chaperone," I teased, rubbing my thumb over the back of her hand.

Her shoulders shook when she laughed. "I know. I wish you could stay the night."

"Same, but I don't know that Quinn's ready for that," I offered. "She's no idiot, but I don't want to dive in too quickly."

I was mentally at peace with taking it slow, but my body had other ideas. "How likely is it that she's gonna burst out and check on us?"

Pink crested on Sasha's cheeks. "Not likely. She watches YouTube and chats with friends. Once she's in her room, she's in."

"Then come here."

Sasha came easily, uncurling her legs as I let go of her hand and slid my hand up her back to lever her closer to me. I didn't count on how difficult it would be to pump the brakes and stop kissing her. One kiss blurred into another and then another.

By the time I managed to break my mouth free of her delicious lips, I was out of breath and my heart was drumming wildly. My cock was swollen to the point of pain.

Dragging my eyes open, I took her in. Her lips were kiss swollen, and her cheeks flushed.

"Fuck me," I rasped.

"No, fuck me," she teased.

I squeezed her hand. "Maybe we should have a lunch date soon?"

Sasha's eyes took on a gleam. "That would be lovely. Quinn is at school during lunch, and she starts back after break on Monday."

"Of course," I whispered against her lips just before kissing her again.

SASHA

Noah was picking me up for lunch. I only had an hour. Although my boss, Helena, would've given me extra time and never really monitored my hours, I had to be back for a meeting.

We were standing on the sidewalk.

"Are you hungry?" His eyes held mine, and the look contained there sent my belly into a big swoop.

I didn't even reply. He turned, reaching for my hand and walking briskly to where his car was parked.

"Where are we going?" I asked as he was pulling away from the curb.

"My place." His tone was almost brusque.

"Are you going to feed me?"

He stopped at a stoplight. When he looked my way, I felt fiery liquid need spin through my veins. This man knew how to give a look. I was hot all over and had to squeeze my thighs together to quell the throb at my core.

"I had something else in mind."

A bubbly sense of joy rose inside, and I laughed as he gunned it when the light turned green. The mix of joy with desire was almost intoxicating.

He reached across the console, his palm landing on my thigh, his touch warm and sure.

"I missed you," he said gruffly.

"It's only been two days," I whispered.

"Two days since I saw you. It's actually been eleven days since we were alone."

I opened my mouth to correct him and then gasped when his hand eased between my thighs. I was wearing a pair of dress slacks.

"I hope you missed me too," he said, his low and gravelly voice sending sparks scattering through me.

I was barely paying attention until he turned down a street only minutes away from where I lived with Quinn. "Oh," I murmured. "You said you were near us."

Noah didn't reply, taking a quick turn onto another street and then pulling into the driveway of an updated, charming colonial home. It was one of those old homes divided into a duplex. With Noah's hand curled around mine, he led me down a walkway to one side. Snow blanketed the area just beyond the path. I took in details as he let me in through the door—dark wood, sunshine spilling through the tall windows, quiet.

Then his mouth was on mine, and our tongues were tangling as we tumbled into a hot, breath-stealing kiss.

He spun me around until I felt the cool wood of the door seeping through my jacket and blouse. Need was pouring through me, and I was frantic to get closer.

"Noah—" I gasped, my head thumping against the door as his lips blazed a hot trail down the side of my neck.

"Yes, love?" he murmured just before nipping my earlobe and sending shivers chasing over my skin.

I didn't know what I wanted, not specifically. I just needed him buried inside me. I craved relief from the need racing through me.

Somehow, I got his pants unbuttoned, letting out a moan when I felt the hot skin of his cock under my touch. Meanwhile, he deftly opened my blouse, and a ragged sigh slipped out when his warm palm cupped a breast. His thumb teased over my achy nipple before he swore and impatiently undid my bra. My fingers speared into his hair when he bent low and brought his mouth over a nipple. Pleasure darted straight to my core. My panties were soaked.

When he shoved them down—when did he get my pants undone?—he teased his fingers into my swollen folds. "Mmm, so wet, you feel so good," he murmured. "Hang on a sec."

In a moment, he'd produced a condom out of his pocket and smoothed it on. He shifted, lifting me against him and guiding himself into position at the cradle of my hips. I felt the thick press of his crown at my entrance and curled my legs around his hips.

"Look at me," he commanded.

My eyelids were heavy, but I dragged them open. We stared at each other as he slowly sank into me, sheathing himself in a gentle slide. He pumped his hips, settling himself more deeply. I bit my lip as my pussy rippled around him.

He held me tight, the door giving him an assist, as he drew back to fill me again. I felt exposed, frantic, and needy. I felt stripped bare as if he could see all my secrets. I wasn't the kind of woman who got desperate for a guy.

Except for Noah, I was.

With his dark eyes on mine, he fucked me slowly against the door. My release started to roll through me, rising in waves, until one crested high, and the froth of pleasure burst through me. I shuddered around him. His lips were on mine, catching my cry just as I felt him go taut, and the heat of his release filled me. It was all over but the gasping.

He pressed hot, open-mouthed kisses along my jaw before lifting his head and brushing my tangled hair away from my face.

"I didn't mean for that to be so—" He stopped abruptly and gave his head a little shake, as if to clear it.

"Rushed, crazy?" I offered hopefully.

He chuckled, slowly withdrawing and easing me to the floor. I instantly missed being joined with him like that. I was almost shocked at my state. He had just given me an explosive orgasm. I was supposed to be at lunch, and instead, I was getting fucked against the door.

He helped me tidy my clothes and then stepped into the bathroom to dispose of the condom, buttoning himself back up as he walked out. "Shall we get takeout on the way back?" he asked.

I was feeling bashful, but I lifted my eyes to him. I didn't want to go back to work. I wanted to play hooky and spend the afternoon with him. See, that girl I'd been in high school, a little bit of her was still inside me, ready to throw caution to the wind and be foolish.

"Sasha?" he prompted.

"Show me your place before we go."

Noah took my hand and led me through. Downstairs was a living room to the front with a beautiful granite fireplace. There was a small study and a kitchen and dining area to the back. He led me up the stairs, where I was surprised to discover three bedrooms off the landing.

"What are you doing with all this space?" I asked when we were on our way out.

He shrugged as he held the door open for me. "I know it's more than I need. Dallas and Audrey live on the other side of the duplex. They got it for a really good deal, so it works for me. It's nice being close to them, and they can use me for babysitting."

A laugh bubbled up. "You babysit?"

He looked genuinely affronted. "Of

course." After we got in the car, he cast me a quick glance. "Maybe I don't have my own kids yet, but I can deal with babysitting."

I didn't know why, but this little detail was endearing. I was already in, well over my head and falling hard and fast, so fast I feared a crash landing. But to hear that he did backup babysitting for his nephew was almost too much. Even worse, it gave me ideas. Ideas I shouldn't have.

When he pulled up in front of my office, he reached into the back seat, handing me the takeout we had picked up. "I promise, the sandwiches are delicious," he assured me.

"I'm sure they are." Although I'd lived in Boston for years, I didn't have the time or the extra spending money to be checking out the endless array of restaurant options. Noah had stopped by a sandwich place only a few minutes away from where I worked, and I'd never been there.

"When can I see you again?" he asked.

Much as I wanted to see him tonight, tomorrow, the following night, and so on, I was almost afraid. I felt like I needed to slow down if only to keep myself sane.

"How about Friday?"

"Today's Monday," he pointed out.

"I know," I said slowly.

He leaned across the seat, palming my cheek and turning my face toward his. Before I could even take a breath, we were in the middle of another mind-bending, breath-stealing kiss. When he drew back, he asked, "Do you still want to wait until Friday?"

My brain cells were scrambled. I bit my lip and shook my head. "Obviously not, but I was trying to be responsible."

"How about Wednesday? We'll split the difference."

I stared into his eyes with my heartbeat echoing. I couldn't help the smile that stretched across my face as I nodded.

Chapter Nineteen

NOAH

"What name?" I asked, glancing over at Cole.

"Jonathon Smith," Cole repeated.

The name was clanging a distant bell in my thoughts, but I couldn't quite place it. I recognized it. Somehow, I knew it was linked to Sasha.

"Let me see it."

Cole spun the file around and slid it across the desk to me. I was a visual person, so reading information clicked more quickly for me. As soon as I read the name, I said, "That's Quinn's father."

"Quinn?" Cole prompted.

"Sasha's daughter."

"Sasha?" he prompted next.

I lifted my eyes to his. I took a breath,

steeling myself to get some hell for this. Cole was a fellow agent in the FBI and friends with Dallas and me. He was married with kids and had teased Dallas mercilessly when Dallas finally got hitched with Audrey. I'd been the odd man out and frankly scoffed at the idea of settling down.

Sasha turned that thinking on its head, which was kind of crazy, all things considered.

"When I went to Haven's Bay for the holidays, I ran into an old friend of Thea's. I might be dating her," I explained, keeping my tone casual.

"Might?" he countered, giving me a skeptical look.

"Okay, I am dating her."

"How am I just hearing about this now?"

"Dude, I've only been back for two weeks. Plus, I paid the usual toll of going on vacation and have been too busy to breathe around here."

We joked that there was a high toll to pay when you went on vacation with mountains of email and paperwork to plow through while also jumping right into whatever cases were active.

Cole chuckled. "Fine. I'll cut you a little slack. Damn. I owe Dallas fifty bucks."

Glancing up, I narrowed my eyes. "For what?"

He grinned. "Whether you'd ever date someone. I said no because you're too cynical. Dallas disagreed and said you'd eventually fall."

I shifted my shoulders as I leaned back in my chair. "Dude, we're just dating."

He shook his head. "Nah. You're the guy who doesn't even do friends with benefits. You keep things so distant that, if you're dating, you seriously like this woman."

My phone rang, and I tapped the button to mute the ringer. "Enough about that. How does this guy tie into the case with Jones?"

"Well, they are both popping up in the trail of people using stolen identities for credit card fraud. The weird part is, they're not doing it personally. It's essentially a pass-through scheme."

"So Quinn's father somehow knows the Jones family?"

Cole shrugged. "Maybe, maybe not. Either way, they're both using the same bank and stolen information to funnel money."

"Fuck."

My friend gave me a considering look. "Not so sure you should stay on this case."

"Why?" I practically barked.

Cole's brows hitched up. "Because it's personal. You also know what Dallas will say," he pointed out.

I did know precisely what my older brother would say. I narrowed my eyes at Cole. "I'll step off the case, but that doesn't mean I'm not gonna look into it on my own."

His mouth kicked up in a grin. "I know that. If I wondered if Sasha meant something to you, now I know."

Chapter Twenty

SASHA

When I got home from work, my brain weary from hours of typing up reports, I dropped my keys in the small bowl on the table by the door and let my purse slide off my shoulder. The soft thump of it on the floor was punctuation for my long day.

Keeping my jacket on, I fetched my gloves out of the closet and switched from my work shoes into my slip-on winter boots before hurrying out to shovel the front stairs. There were three apartments in the building, separate from Melanie's. We were all pretty good about taking turns to shovel the outside stairs when it snowed. It was finally slowing after dropping almost six inches during the day. The porch light glowed in the snowy darkness as I shoveled.

For some reason, shoveling was an activity that tended to elicit feelings of loneliness for me. I thought it was because the first apartment I had when Quinn was a baby was an upstairs apartment with its own entrance to the side. While I didn't mind shoveling, it had always been me clearing those steps alone and forever feeling tired. Being a single mother with a baby was a blur of exhaustion. These days, I wasn't as tired as I used to be because Quinn slept through the night, which meant I did too. But, still, the feeling lingered.

After I was done, I propped the shovel in the corner of the porch and kicked the snow off my boots before hurrying back upstairs. I shed my coat and boots, my eyes doing a quick check to see Quinn's laptop on the kitchen counter. Some nights, she was already done with her homework when I got home, and on others, she would return to the kitchen table after dinner and finish.

Her bedroom door was closed, which wasn't unusual. I changed out of my work clothes into a comfy pair of fleece pants and a fuzzy top. I wanted to be warm and comfortable. I idly wondered what Noah was doing this evening and imagined him in his office working. I didn't even know what his office looked like. By his own admission, I knew work was his life for the most part.

I experienced a twinge of longing, wishing he was here to curl up on the couch and watch a show with me. I shook that away because I was starving and needed to make sure Quinn had something for dinner. Pausing by her door, I knocked lightly, calling, "Quinn?"

I was greeted with silence. When I knocked again, her voice was muffled when she replied, "Come in."

Opening the door, I found her sitting on her bed with her legs crossed. Her phone lay on the bed in front of her as she stared down at it. Her hands were twisted together in her lap.

Her brow was pinched with worry, and I abruptly had a hollow feeling in my stomach.

Crossing the room quickly, I slipped my hips on the bed beside her. "What is it?"

I resisted the urge to pick up her phone. She lifted her eyes to mine. "My father sent me an email." I stared at her blankly, my brain not computing. She repeated, "My father, better known as my sperm donor."

"Oh. Oh!" Finally, the information processed. "Really?"

Quinn nodded slowly, blinking and swallowing audibly.

"What did he say, honey?"

"He wanted to know how I was doing." My daughter spoke slowly, almost as if she were picking her way through her feelings about it.

My fingers practically itched to grab her phone. I resisted the urge, lacing my fingers together, almost as if to force them to behave.

"How do you feel?" I pressed, trying to keep the spinning sense of panic and worry out of my voice.

Quinn's eyes whipped up to mine. "Angry. He's known I existed for years. Why is he reaching out to me now?"

A confusing mix of anger, disappointment, and raw sadness tightened my chest. When one parent completely ignored the existence of their child, it was hard to know how to handle it when they reached out. In my case, I'd always been just getting by, so the idea that my stupid high school boyfriend might come out of nowhere and try to get custody of Quinn terrified me. But it also hurt me that he didn't even care enough to try to be a part of my daughter's life. She was an incredible girl, the best ever, and he didn't even know it.

"Sweetie—" I began, again stopping abruptly when Quinn shook her head sharply.

"Mom, it doesn't matter. He's an asshole."

"It's okay if it *does* matter," I added as I shifted closer to her on the bed and curled my arm around her shoulders.

She tucked her head into the side of my neck, and I could feel the little tremor running through her.

"I wish it didn't get to me," she mumbled into my collarbone.

"It's okay that it does," I said, circling my palm on her back.

After a moment, she lifted her head and straightened her shoulders. My arm fell away as I looked at her. Her chin rose slightly, and I bit back the urge to smile. She was feeling stubborn.

"I'm just going to let his email wait. He's been in no rush to talk to me, so I'm not in any hurry to respond to him."

I suspected he'd known how to contact her. A few years ago when her grandmother had reached out, I'd given her an email for Quinn with Quinn's permission. He must've gotten that email address from her.

"What's for dinner?" she asked, straightening her legs and wiggling her feet.

"I was just going to take a look and see what we have. Any requests?"

"Can we get pizza delivered?"

A sharp pain pierced my heart. Pizza was one of her favorite comfort foods. I knew she was trying to be brave, but her father's email was getting to her.

"Absolutely. Do you want to call and order?"

She shimmied off the bed, and I stood, following her out toward the living room. Phone in hand, she nodded. "Of course."

A pizza place only a few blocks away was always quick with delivery. Quinn ordered our favorite—half pepperoni and half Greek. While I emptied the dishwasher, she sat at the kitchen table, opening her laptop and starting her homework.

I was going to check that email later and decide whether to email her dad myself. Just as I thought I wouldn't bother talking about it again, I decided I needed to tell her I might do that. I knew trying to keep it from her wouldn't be a good plan because she'd probably find out.

"Sweetie," I began, turning after I put away the last dish. She glanced up from her laptop, her hands stilling on the keyboard. I continued, "Can you forward me that email?"

Quinn was silent for a second, and I was afraid she was annoyed, or even angry, that I was injecting myself between them. After a few beats, she shrugged. "Sure. I figured you'd want to see it. Are you going to reply to him?"

"I'm not sure. I might. If I do, I promise I'll tell you, and I'll show you what I say," I said carefully.

She blinked, pushing her glasses up on her nose. "Okay."

Later that night, after we enjoyed pizza and Quinn went to bed, I leaned my head against my headboard, contemplating asking Noah for his opinion on what to do about Quinn's father reaching out to her. While I craved some feedback because the entire situation felt fraught, the idea made me nervous for reasons I didn't quite understand. I finally concluded it was because I was so accustomed to doing all of this alone.

I lifted my phone off the nightstand beside my bed, quickly texting Noah. I really needed some advice, and I trusted him.

Me: *Quinn's father emailed her. I don't know what to think. I need someone to tell me to be reasonable and not panic about this.*

My thumbs hovered over the screen as I hesitated to hit send. As if my thumb knew better than my brain, it tapped the send button before I could dwell on it.

Lowering the phone, I let it fall to my lap. Seconds later, I felt the vibration on my side and glanced down to see Noah was calling me. I experienced a rushed mix of emotions. Relief because I really needed some advice, joy because he reached out that quickly, and a subtle hum of anxiety. Not specifically of Noah, but about letting anyone matter too much.

I swiped my thumb across the screen and lifted the phone to my ear. "Hello?"

"Hey. What are you doing?"

The warm lilt in his voice curled around my heart, easing the thrumming tension. A tension I'd been holding tightly inside ever since Quinn told me her father had emailed her.

"Trying not to overthink," I said flatly and honestly, letting out a frazzled sigh.

"When did he email her?"

Noah's tone shifted to solemn and serious, and I could practically feel the gears turning in his brain.

"Just today. She forwarded it to me. Do you want me to send it to you?"

"That would be—" He paused abruptly. "I'd like for you to send it to me, but I want to make sure that's okay with Quinn."

Impatience jostled in my thoughts, followed immediately by gratitude. Wow. This man was already knocking down my defenses. To have him consider my daughter's feelings first, well, it just made me feel all gooey and warm inside.

"You're too good," I finally said softly.

"I'm practical," he said with a low chuckle. "I can imagine she'd be furious if it wasn't okay with her. But tell me what it said."

"Give me a sec."

Pulling the phone away from my ear, I snagged my earbuds where they sat on my nightstand and put them in before plugging them in to the phone, so I could talk and listen while I pulled up my email.

A moment later, I read the email aloud to him.

Hi Quinn. It's your father. I know you haven't heard from me, and I can imagine you're wondering why I'm reaching out now. I want to meet you, if only to apologize for not being involved in your life up to this point. You can reach me at this email or this phone number.

I didn't bother reciting the number.

"It's benign enough," Noah offered after a moment of silence.

"I know, but why now?"

He was quiet for long enough then that I sensed something was up. "What?" I pressed.

"This is just weird. I'm gonna have to talk to Dallas, but Jonathon's name showed up in the investigation we're handling right now. Because of it, I won't be officially on the investigation going forward."

"What?! Do you think him reaching out to her has something to do with this?"

"Maybe, maybe not. The timing is strange."

"What's the investigation about?"

I could feel his hesitation vibrating through the phone line. "Noah, please tell me. I won't tell Quinn. I just want to make sure she's okay and keep her safe."

"His name popped up in a case relating to identity theft and money laundering. That's it. It could be completely benign, and frankly, he could be a victim. This email may not even be from him if that's the case. I'm sure you've already gone over all the safety issues related to online stuff, but it never hurts to chat about it again. I'll talk to Dallas and ask if he's comfortable talking with you and her. I think he will be because he'd want to interview you both. It might be him, or it might be Cole. He's another agent and a good friend of mine."

My heart was thumping unsteadily, and dread coated the insides of my stomach. I took a quick breath.

"Noah—" I began, my words stuttering to a stop because I didn't know what I meant to say. I just wanted my worry to ease.

"Do you want me to come over?" he asked, his voice low.

A rush of emotion swelled inside, tears pricking hot in the back of my eyes. Not because I was sad, but rather because it was startling how easily he was attuned to me. I needed comfort, and I wanted him to be the one to give it to me. And I so, *so* very much wanted to fall asleep wrapped in his strong embrace.

"I want you to, but it's late, and then there will be things to explain to Quinn in the morning."

"I know. I can't wait until I can be there, but I know we need to take it at the pace that's right for her."

After we got off the phone, my thoughts chased each other in circles. I was worried about Quinn's father contacting her and I was missing Noah.

Chapter Twenty-One

NOAH

Quinn's eyes were round behind her glasses when she looked from me to her mother and back again. "Why?" she asked. Her gaze lingered on me, narrowing in suspicion.

"Because your father's name appeared in an investigation. That doesn't mean he's done anything wrong, and in fact, his identity may have been stolen. I have permission to tell you that, so I am. I don't want your mother to forward that email unless it's okay with you. It was originally sent to you," I pointed out.

Quinn pushed her glasses up on her nose, rolling her eyes. "Like I didn't know that," she said pointedly. "I'll forward it to you. What's your email?" She was all business now, sliding her phone out of her pocket and tapping on the screen.

I quickly recited my email address, and she tapped it in. "There." Her eyes lifted to mine. "Make sure it made it."

She looked at me expectantly, so I obediently pulled my phone out of my jacket pocket and checked my email. In a second, her email appeared. "It's there. Thank you. Have you replied to him yet?"

Quinn shook her head quickly, the ponytail on top of her head swinging back and forth. "I thought I'd wait until you tell me it's okay. After Mom said you wanted to ask me, it seemed best to wait."

"You don't have to wait," I replied.

She shrugged. "I'd rather. If someone is being squirrelly and pretending they're him, I'd rather know that. And if it is him, well, geez, he's never going to win dad of the year."

Figuring it was best if I didn't agree with that, I simply said, "Well, whatever you choose to do, if you could keep your mom and me in the loop, that would be great."

"Sure thing, FBI," Quinn deadpanned as she spun away to open the refrigerator.

When I risked a glance at Sasha, her lips were tight at the corners, and I knew she was trying not to laugh.

"Where are you two lovebirds going out to dinner?" Quinn tossed over her shoulder. Leaning into the fridge, she pulled out a container of juice and proceeded to fetch a glass from the cabinet and fill it.

I finally chuckled. "We haven't decided yet. Any requests for takeout?"

Quinn returned the bottle of juice to the refrigerator before turning around and resting her hips against the counter as she glanced between us. Sasha's cheeks had gone pink as soon as Quinn described us as lovebirds.

"That calzone was good, and so was the Thai food. I trust you now, so make it somewhere good and new. We need to expand our eating horizons," she said.

"Okay then, your mom and I will decide. Glad to know you trust my opinion on food."

Quinn shrugged nonchalantly. "You've done well so far, so don't screw it up. Now, I need to go do my homework." She pushed away from the counter. "What time will you be home, Mom?" she asked when she stopped in the archway leading out to the living room.

"Before bedtime," Sasha replied quickly.

"Are you spending the night?" Quinn's eyes bounced to me.

My brain stalled at that question. The silence in the room felt loaded.

"Quinn!" Sasha sputtered.

Quinn pursed her lips and rolled her eyes. "I'm not stupid. You two spent a whole week alone together over the Christmas holidays. Don't even try to pretend you didn't get it on."

I wasn't much of a blusher, but wow, Quinn knocked me back on my heels, and I felt the heat creep up my neck.

Her eyes moved to me. "You seem like you really like my mom." Suddenly, she wasn't joking. "If you hurt her, I'll make things really uncomfortable for you. But it's okay if you spend the night. I'm not gonna freak out about it." A teasing hint entered her tone again.

At that, she twirled away, waving her fingers over her shoulder. "I've got homework to do. I'll be in my room."

Sasha and I waited in silence until her door clicked shut. Sasha sagged into a chair by the kitchen table. "Oh, my God," she said slowly.

"She seems to enjoy embarrassing us."

"She enjoys trying to make adults feel foolish," Sasha offered with a shrug.

I crossed the kitchen to stop in front of

her, resting my hands on either side of the table, caging her in my arms. "It's fine. She's just being a teenager. I feel like I just won something," I murmured, right before dipping my head and brushing my lips over Sasha's.

"What did you win?" she whispered when I lifted my head.

"Permission to spend the night."

Chapter Twenty-Two

SASHA

I came to a conclusion during dinner that night with Noah: foreplay didn't require touching. It was bad enough already with my response to Noah. I constantly felt as if my body was an engine being revved. One look from him, not even purposeful, and it was like a heavy foot on the gas pedal, sending my desire hurtling forward.

He took me to a small café, nothing fancy. He said they had delicious pot pies. Quinn's faith in his ability to choose restaurants was well placed because the pot pies were heavenly. It was, as he put it, really an English pub tucked in a corner of Boston. The food was absolutely delicious and perfect for a brisk, clear night in February.

"How was work?" he asked after the server, a matronly woman who clearly knew Noah, had checked with us.

With her warm gaze and questions, I felt as if I were being appraised, but I didn't really mind. Noah was worth having friends who protected him.

I shrugged. "Work was busy, but I like it that way. She's kind of protective of you," I observed as the server paused by the next table.

"Norma?" Noah returned, his brows hitching up in surprise.

"Yes, in a good way. It's obvious she cares and doesn't want anyone to take advantage of you." I chuckled to myself.

"What's so funny?" Noah prompted.

"As if I would be slick enough to take advantage." I rolled my eyes.

"You underestimate yourself." His low tone sent heat skating over my skin.

"What do you mean? I'm barely treading water in this, you know? I haven't had much of a social life, and even less of a dating life."

"Because you've been busy being a mom." He dipped his chin. "As you should be. Quinn is delightful, and it's obvious she loves you."

Many men didn't know all you had to do to get a single mother to swoon was say something like that. My pride for Quinn ran deep. I loved her fiercely and wanted nothing more than for her to be happy. To have someone notice what a great kid she was, well, it warmed my heart in the best possible way.

I swallowed. "Thank you. Obviously, I love her to pieces." Anxiety suddenly struck a discordant chord in my heart. "How worried do we need to be about whatever this investigation is?"

He reached across the table, curling his hand over mine. "I want to tell you that you don't need to worry, but that would be a lie. I can tell you the investigation has nothing to do with violence. White collar crime is rather mundane. It can ruin lives, but only by screwing with people's financial stability. I'm mostly worried about making sure no one steals her identity. Separate from that, I'm obviously worried that her father doesn't hurt her, emotionally speaking."

I took a quick breath and nodded. "Okay. Dallas will keep you up to speed?"

Noah had already explained he couldn't stay on the investigation because of his connection to Quinn. "Of course. I'll be there tomorrow when you two come by the office."

"Good."

Just then, Norma arrived with our check. Her eyes dropped to where our hands were joined and resting on the table. "You be good to her, Noah," she said with a kind smile.

I had to bite my lip to keep from laughing when Noah looked up at her. "Sasha told me she thought you were protective. You know I wouldn't bring anyone here who I didn't completely trust. We grew up together in Haven's Bay in Maine. It's been a while, but you don't need to worry."

Norma's cheeks plumped up with her smile when she looked at me. "I had a good feeling about you, and I told my Norm I thought Noah had a tendre for you."

I smiled, ignoring the heat flaring in my cheeks. "Well, thank you. That's good to know," I finally said.

Norma set the check down on the table. "I hope the food was good."

"It was delicious. I'm so glad Noah brought me here." She set down a paper bag containing the takeout we had ordered for Quinn. "I hope your daughter enjoys it too. Noah, you come back soon." She squeezed his shoulder before she hurried off.

I looked over at him. "Norma and Norm?"

He flashed a quick grin. "Yup. Go figure.

I guess it was meant to be."

A few minutes later, we were back in the car, and he was deftly navigating through the late evening traffic when he spoke. "I hope you know how much you mean to me."

His eyes flicked to mine briefly, the look there hot enough to singe me. It also held an intensity of emotion I didn't know how to interpret. My heart thrashed inside my chest, and my mouth went dry. I swallowed, taking the moment to absorb his profile, the clean strong lines. I loved him. The pure truth struck me. It felt as if a bracing gust of wind lifted me, and my feet slammed to the ground as I stumbled from the force.

"What do you mean?" I finally asked, my voice coming out a little ragged.

His hand reached across the console, lacing his fingers into mine. "I mean, Sasha, that I'm falling for you. I already told you that, but I don't think you believed me."

"It feels rushed like it doesn't make sense. I told you my life isn't all fun and games. I don't know how you can know that until there's been at least a few teenage melt-downs, and I'm stressing about bills."

His gaze slid to mine again, and he shook his head just slightly. "Sasha, we've known each other for years. Maybe we lost touch, but it's not like this is fresh. I get it. We don't have to hurry. I'll wait for a few teenage melt-downs, and you can stress about bills. Al-though I wish you wouldn't. If you need help—"

I cut him off fast. "I don't need you to ride into my life and make it easy. It's impor-tant to me that I can support Quinn and myself."

"I know." His fingers squeezed mine.

My heart kept pounding as we rode the rest of the way home in silence. It wasn't an uncomfortable silence, more of a potent silence.

When Noah approached the house, I said, "You could park in the driveway behind my car if you want."

I felt his smile before I even saw it. Glancing over, I laughed when he said, "I was wondering if I still had permission. Quinn gave it to me, but you hadn't yet."

I was absorbing his words when he put his car in park and cut the engine. When he turned to me, the look in his eyes was fierce. My belly swooped, and need throbbed at the apex of my thighs.

He leaned over, palming my cheek as he brought his lips to mine. I literally felt elec-tricity sizzle from that point of contact straight to my core. It pulled tight like a string as my body vibrated. His tongue glided against mine in a quick, sensual tease before he drew away.

"Quinn might be awake," I said breathlessly.

"I can deal. Patience is a virtue," he teased as I unbuckled my seat belt.

I laughed. "Your mom used to say that."

I heard the click of his seatbelt buckle, and then his touch brushed against my hip. He lifted my seat belt so it didn't tangle on my arm. The subtle gesture felt protective.

I had just gathered up my purse from the floor when the cold air washed in as he opened the door for me. Noah was that kind of man. He insisted on me getting over some things. I was so used to pushing through life and taking care of myself that it almost made me feel a little uncomfortable.

His hand rested on the curve of my spine as we walked up the stairs inside. Our footsteps echoed when we crested the landing on the second floor. The door across from mine opened, and Melanie peered out. "Oh, hi," she said, trying to act all surprised.

I knew it was a ruse because she could see the driveway from her living room window. Melanie wasn't very subtle and was absolutely nosy. I didn't mind. It was good to have friends who cared.

Noah simply smiled. He had the kind of smile that put anyone at ease. It was gracious and polite with a hint of a twinkle in his eye. "Well, what a surprise to see you, Melanie." He was going to play along.

Her eyes sparkled with her return smile, and I could tell she was enjoying it. "What did you bring Quinn tonight?" she asked, her gaze darting down to the paper bag held in Noah's hand.

"A delicious new place. Well, it's not new, but it's new to me. It's like an old British pub, and they make yummy meat pies and sandwiches. I should've thought to bring you something," I commented.

"No worry, dear," she said with an airy wave. "Next time we have lunch, why don't we go there?"

"Perfect," I replied.

"Good night," she said. Just as she was about to close the door, she peered out again. "And, don't worry, you can park there all night." She winked at Noah before disappearing.

My cheeks were hot. I eyed him and mouthed, "Sorry."

He smiled and pressed a kiss to my temple. A moment later, we were in my apartment. "I adore Melanie, but she's nosy."

"Sasha, I don't care at all," he said flatly. "In fact, I'm glad you have a good neighbor who checks on you." We hung our coats and took off our shoes. "Quinn doesn't seem up," he observed.

I arched a brow. "Just because we can't hear her doesn't mean she's asleep. Let me check and see if she's awake."

I walked down the short hallway, hearing the low hum of what had to be her phone or computer. She loved streaming things on her devices rather than watching television unless that was something we did together.

"Quinn," I called through her door. "Are you hungry?"

I heard Noah's low chuckle from the kitchen at the sound of her hopping off her bed and opening her door.

"How was dinner?" she asked cheerfully as she skipped down the hall and into the kitchen.

Following her, I offered, "Delicious."

Noah was already opening the bag for her and handing it over. "What's this?" She peered in and looked back up expectantly.

"A meat pie. Your mom said you like steak. It's a British thing. They call it a pie, but it's sort of like a pastry sandwich. Very old-school. They even make ones that have sweet on one side and savory on the other. Apparently, that's what farmers used to take out in the fields when they were working all day."

Quinn loved history and smiled brightly at that little nugget of information. "Thank you. Can I eat in my room?"

"Of course. Just put your plate in the sink after," I replied.

"I'm not taking a plate," she said with a saucy grin. "I already have water." She glanced at Noah. "I'm only allowed to have water in my bedroom since I have a habit of spilling things. This is made to eat without a plate." Sliding on her socks over to my side with the paper bag in hand, she pecked me on the cheek. "Good night."

At that, my teenage daughter was gone in a flash, the sound of her bedroom door closing behind her punctuating the end of that interaction.

I was suddenly and unaccountably nervous. Although I had obviously been with Noah more than once by this point, this was the very first time I'd had a man spend the night with my daughter in the house. My few ventures into dating hadn't ever gotten serious. I'd never actually brought anyone to my house. This felt oddly momentous.

When I met his gaze, his eyes softened. In another second, he was right in front of me, reaching for my hands. I was twisting my fingers tightly together, a cue to how anxious I was.

"I don't have to stay," he murmured.

I blinked and took a deep breath. "I don't know why I'm freaking out."

Tucking my forehead into the curve of his neck, I found his scent comforting. He was always warm and smelled a little crisp with a spicy hint underneath. As I breathed him in, I realized something. My comfort with him and simply telling him how I felt answered all of my questions. I didn't know how this would play out, but my feelings were real and true. It felt as if I had tapped into a spring deep in my being, one I'd forgotten, with emotions rushing forth.

Noah was right. We *did* know each other, even if we were relearning each other and forming a new connection.

Lifting my head, I met his eyes. "No. I want you to stay."

Then I took him by the hand and led him into my bedroom, across the hallway from Quinn's.

Chapter Twenty-Three

NOAH

My need had been humming through my body all evening. I'd been keeping it on a tight leash, but my cock was swollen to the point of aching. It didn't help to have Sasha wearing a silky blouse where the top button was just low enough that I could see the shadowed valley between the soft curves of her breasts. At one point, she lifted her hand to brush her hair off her shoulder, and the silk slid to the side, just enough for my eyes to play peekaboo with the navy blue lace hiding there.

When the bedroom door clicked shut behind us, I spun her around and pressed her against it. There was a low hum in her throat and a little hitch in her breath, the sounds driving spurs in the flanks of my need.

Her eyes met mine, dark with need. "I think you have a thing for doors," she murmured, her tone sultry and teasing.

I shook my head, dipping low until my lips brushed over hers as I answered, "It's not the doors. It's you. You make me too impatient to get much farther than the door."

I could feel the heat of her arousal at the apex of her thighs as I pressed flush against her and fit my mouth over hers. I needed this kiss on a cellular level. Raw, pure, elemental desire was sizzling through me and scrambling every synapse in my brain.

Sasha met me with bold, teasing strokes of her tongue, the little sounds in her throat driving me absolutely fucking wild as our kiss went deeper. I devoured her mouth, laying claim to it with as much fervor as I wanted to love her. By the time our lips broke apart, we were both breathless, gasping for air.

Sasha blinked up at me, pressing a palm to my chest, just over my heart. "We're going to have to keep the volume down," she whispered.

While her words weren't intended to be sexy, her throaty, husky voice was. My hips rocked against hers, restless to slake the pressure of my arousal.

"Okay," I murmured, reluctantly stepping back from her bedroom door.

I had just enough sense to dimly realize that the door was the closest to Quinn's bedroom across the hall. As much as I wanted to take Sasha right then and there, maybe a few extra feet were warranted.

Sasha shimmied out from between me and the door, catching one of my hands in hers as I turned. I took in her bedroom. There was nothing remarkable about it, except that it was hers. My gaze took in a queen-sized bed piled high with pillows and a fluffy silvery-gray down quilt. A square purple rug lay on the hardwood floor at the foot of her bed with a dresser to one side and a small night table on the other.

On the wall hung a photo of Haven's Bay. Maine's rugged and beautiful coastline showed off in Haven's Bay with rocky cliffs on one side that shifted to a sandy beach on the other. It was a sunset photo, and the shimmer of red, orange, and gold in the sky was reflected in the water in the bay. The boats in the harbor looked stately and beautiful under the setting sun.

"Haven's Bay," I murmured.

Sasha nodded. "I always loved that photo."

The brief respite from the need galloping through me ended when she gave my hand a little tug. When I turned to face her, she leaned up, and this time, she took the lead with another kiss. I forgot where I was. Hell, I forgot everything but the feel of her lips and tongue teasing mine. In a hot second, her naughty fingers unbuttoned my jeans, and her silky palm dipped into my boxers. She shoved my jeans down just enough for my cock to spring free.

In another fiery second, her silky palm curled around my length, and my cock leaped under her touch. She murmured something, and I felt her thumb sliding over the tip, which was slippery from the pre-cum already dripping out of me.

Fuck me. Sasha had no idea just how completely she held me in her thrall. Heat blazed through me, the snapping fire engulfing me when she knelt, and I felt her warm mouth close over my thick crown. My hand tangled in her hair when she sucked me in. I gasped her name. She lifted her head long enough to say, "Be quiet."

Jesus. Taking orders from Sasha was easy, except that one. I had to grit my teeth to contain the raw pleasure trying to rip loose in my throat. She sucked me in again and pumped me lightly in her grip, her fist slick from her mouth.

Scrambling to get some control, I tugged lightly on her hair where I'd laced my fingers. She lifted her head, and I bit out, "I need to be inside you."

Our clothes came off in a blur, tossed this way and that on the floor. A moment later, Sasha was shimmying back on the bed, and I caught her ankle lightly. She froze, her eyes locking with mine when she looked up. She was naked, her breasts rising and falling with the rapid gusts of her breath. Her nipples were tight little peaks, dusky deep pink under the light cast from a lamp beside her bed. One of her knees had fallen out to the side, and I could see her pussy—pink, glistening, and swollen.

My cock throbbed. I had wisely already rolled a condom on as soon as I kicked my jeans off. "I need to taste you," I murmured, my voice low, almost guttural.

I slid my palm up her thigh, savoring as her other knee fell to the side when I leaned over. I breathed in her scent—musky, sweet, and salty. I licked into her, once and then again. She cried out, her hips rolling into my mouth. I lifted my head just as I sank two fingers inside her core. She let out a moan.

"Be quiet," I parried her words back at her.

"Noah," she pleaded. "Please, I need you."

Well, when she said it like that, there was only one thing to do. I rose, the mattress giving under my weight as I came down over her. Propping myself on my elbows, I brushed her tangled hair away from her face and kissed her as the tip of my cock teased at her slippery wet entrance.

She gasped into my mouth. I sheathed myself in her silky, clenching heat in one slow slide until I was buried to the root. Her pussy rippled around me, and I almost came. I clenched my teeth and dragged my eyes open. I needed to see her.

"Noah," she panted, her hips bucking against me. "I need—"

I drew back and thrust forward in one swift surge, filling her completely and savoring her raspy cry. She bit her lip to try to stay quiet. A few more strokes, and I could feel her climax coming as her body began to tremble and her channel clamped tighter and tighter around me. My release was threatening, sizzling like lightning and fire at the base of my spine as my balls tightened.

My name came out in a choked cry as she shuddered roughly when I buried myself once more. Then it was all over but for the shudders of my own body and my release rolling through me in waves. I was spent by the time it was over and collapsed against her. I shifted quickly, rolling so she rested half on top of me.

We lay there together, my heartbeat echoing through my body as my breath slowed. Sasha's skin was damp against mine, and I sifted my fingers through her hair.

I did not want to leave her side, but I had to ask the question.

"Should I go for the night?"

Chapter Twenty-Four

SASHA

I felt boneless as pleasure continued to ping through my body. I heard the rumble of Noah's words against my ear where I lay on his chest. It took an effort to lift my head. I curled my hand into a fist and rested my chin on it. His eyes were intent as they searched mine.

"Is that a responsibility question?" I asked. His brows hitched up. "That's what I say to Quinn when she's asking me something about being responsible," I clarified. "I don't want you to go. Do you feel like you should because Quinn's here?"

He shook his head. "Not really, but if you thought so, then I would drag my ass out of this bed, kiss you good night, and very reluctantly leave."

His answer delighted me, and I giggled, dipping my head and pressing a kiss in the divot at the base of his throat. "I think she can handle tonight. Plus, that gives us more time."

When Noah's lips curled into a slow smile, my belly flipped, and my heart felt exposed. This man *slayed* me in more ways than one.

"More?" he prompted.

"Yes, more."

What began as a teasing moment, suddenly felt deeply intimate. I knew the surface of our words was about sex and the chemistry that felt like a fire bomb in the sky, but the undercurrent was *all* emotion. I was falling so deeply for this man that I didn't know what to think. I feared my efforts to take it slow and do something like a sensible adult were all for naught.

"It's more, and that's all that matters," he murmured, his words spinning around my heart and cinching tightly.

And so it was that Noah fell asleep beside me with my daughter across the hallway for the first time in my life. It felt exactly right. And that terrified me.

———

When I woke the next morning, I heard the shower running and smelled coffee. I wondered if Noah had left already. For a split second, I wondered if the night had been a dream. We'd fallen asleep together. Later, I'd woken up with him curled up behind me and felt the hot press of his arousal against my bottom.

He'd teased me to another climax with his fingers before lifting my thigh and sliding into me from behind. He'd fucked me slowly in the darkness, unraveling me until I trembled with pleasure and had to bury my cries in the pillow.

When I moved after waking, I felt the twinges of soreness, of being loved so thoroughly. When I stretched my arm out to the side, the sheets were still warm, so I knew he'd only recently gotten up, perhaps moments earlier.

I lay there for another minute, cradling the memories of last night like a gift inside my heart. I also needed to scramble up some courage. Because now I had to face Quinn. With Noah here. In the morning.

I heard the shower turn off. With a sigh, I kicked the covers back and got up, tugging on my around-the-house sweatpants and a comfy fleece top. I splashed water on my face and brushed my teeth in the still steamy bathroom. Padding down the hallway a few minutes later, I found Noah pouring a cup of coffee and Quinn at the kitchen table. She had a bowl of oatmeal in front of her and was already showered. Noah's hair was freshly damp and his cheeks still a little flushed, so I surmised he was the one who had the water running moments ago.

Quinn glanced up. For a split second, she looked so young that my palm flew to my chest. She didn't have her glasses on, and her eyes were bright. She smiled. "Morning, Mom," she said in a sing-song voice. "Noah made me oatmeal, and it's good."

He chuckled. "Why, thank you." His eyes bounced to mine. His gaze was warm and felt intimate, as if he was unwrapping the layers around my heart, right here, in a matter of seconds, in front of my daughter. "Coffee?" he asked lightly.

"Yes, please," I managed, lifting my chin and crossing over to slip into the chair across from Quinn. My eyes landed on the paper bag from the restaurant last night. "Did you like the pie?"

Quinn's eyes brightened. "Yes. Next time

you go, I want one of the savory and sweet ones. How come that's not an American thing? There are surely enough English people who settled here," she offered between oatmeal bites.

I felt Noah sit beside me and push a cup of coffee over. My heart flipped over again. I curled both hands around the mug because I needed something to hold on to.

I took a swallow as Noah replied, "Next time we go, you could go with us. We can even go this weekend if you'd like."

Quinn looked back and forth between us. I sipped my coffee and tried to act like this was no big deal. Ever since she was born, I'd told myself I wouldn't get serious with someone until I trusted them completely. I knew what my heart wanted, but, sweet hell, I was diving into the deep end on this with Noah.

"Okay," she finally said. "But I don't want to crash a date."

My cheeks got hot, and I gulped my coffee, relieved when she took another bite of oatmeal. I felt Noah's hand slide on my thigh and give it a gentle squeeze. God, I could really get used to waking up like this.

"You're not crashing a date," Noah said

calmly. "How about this weekend? Norma would love to meet you."

Quinn's eyes were sharp when she looked up, her gaze flicking back and forth between us. "Who is Norma?"

"One of the owners," I replied. "Norma and Norm own the place if you can believe that. I didn't have the pleasure of meeting Norm, but Norma was very nice."

She thought that was hysterical and burst out laughing. The morning rolled on. Quinn left for school, and Noah offered to take me to work, adding, "Plus, we need to pick up Quinn from school so Dallas can talk with her. I'd like for us all to be there."

My lips were saying "okay" before I could even contemplate it. It was a practical suggestion, but then I worried that Noah would be bringing me home, and I'd want him to stay. My mind loved debating anxiety-fueled topics. It often felt like a tennis game in my brain.

Chapter Twenty-Five

NOAH

My brother eyed me from across his desk, a sardonic glint in his eyes. "Do you want to sit in?" he asked dryly.

"Yes."

"I think it's best if you don't," he said, his words measured as his gaze sobered.

"Not as an agent, just a supportive—" I cut myself off abruptly.

Dallas's lips curled into a sly smile as he chuckled. "A supportive what?"

Leaning back in my chair, I let out a low chuckle and ran a hand through my hair. "Friend?" I offered helpfully.

"If you think you're just Sasha's friend, you're more of an idiot than I thought," my brother countered, all humor leaving his eyes.

"I know I'm not just her friend. Is this officially an interview, anyway?" I pressed.

Dallas shook his head. "I just want to take a look at that email. Sasha forwarded it, but since Quinn's willing to let us look at the laptop, I want to see what else I can trace from it. Since you're wondering, I'll let you know. It doesn't look like Quinn's father has been involved. As far as we can tell, it looks like his ID was stolen. He's not a criminal, but he is in a bit of a jam."

"What do you mean?" Unease slithered down my spine.

"He likes to gamble. That's all. Nothing sinister, nothing even illegal. Unless remarkably poor judgment combined with a propensity to bet when he doesn't have the financing to do so is criminal."

"Fuck," I muttered. "Do you think this means Quinn and Sasha are unsafe?"

Dallas shook his head quickly. "Oh no. If they had money, perhaps, but they don't. I'm more curious to see where Quinn's father's trail will lead us as far as getting more on the guys running this massive laundering scheme. I've already interviewed him. He knows he made some dumb decisions, and this may be the first time in his life that he's facing actual accountability for them. He's fully cooperating."

I didn't realize how tense I was until I sagged into the chair, the tension bundled in the muscles along the back of my shoulders loosening for the first time in days. "Why do you think he reached out to Quinn?"

"He claims he didn't. So your guess was right. Someone's using him, not to get to Quinn, but to rattle him."

"Fuck."

Dallas stood from his desk, crossing over to a small table against the wall and pouring himself a cup of coffee from the coffee pot. "Would you like some?" He threw his question over his shoulder.

"Please."

A moment later, he handed me a cup of black coffee before sitting down at his desk again. I took a gulp, savoring the rich flavor. We were lucky in the office here. One of the admin assistants made damn good coffee. He tended to circle through the offices periodically throughout the day, making sure we all had fresh coffee. Dallas and I sat in silence for a few moments while we sipped our drinks.

I contemplated my usual busy schedule. I

tended to work a lot and not mind it. Now, I wanted time with Sasha and Quinn. Even though I wasn't with Sasha every night, I didn't want the adrenaline-driven exhaustion that came with working all the time. I had something to look forward to, something else to focus on. Specifically, two someones— Sasha and Quinn. I didn't even know how to absorb the emotion attached to two of them. There were my feelings for Sasha, which were independent of Quinn, yet not. Because Quinn was Sasha's first priority. As such, she had become mine as well in a very short span of time.

"You're in love." Dallas spoke with casual confidence.

My eyes whipped to his just as my heart gave a rattling kick in my chest, almost as if it were a gong sounding its agreement.

I took another swallow from my mug, trying to steady myself. "Do you think?" I returned with practiced nonchalance in my tone.

"I don't think, I *know*. How are things going?"

I blinked at him, both relieved and disappointed that he didn't press me to agree with him. Now *that* was something to wonder about. While I was already coming to terms with just how quickly Sasha occupied the whole of my heart, I hadn't yet put a label on it. The adjustment psychologically for me was big. My career has taken up so much space for so long.

"Good, I think," I said slowly. "I think Sasha thinks we're moving too fast."

Dallas waved a hand dismissively in the air. "You've known her since we were kids."

"That's what I told her. There's Quinn too."

Dallas looked thoughtful. "Of course. What's Quinn like?"

An image of Sasha's self-assured, quirky daughter flashed in my thoughts—her dark hair, her eyes, so much like Sasha's behind those big glasses, her sense of humor, and the youthfulness she exuded. Like most teenagers, she was both wise and young at once.

Before I could reply, there was a light knock on the office door. John, the very admin assistant who made great coffee, poked his head in the door. "Your appointment is here."

"Send them on back," Dallas replied.

"I guess you'll see what Quinn is like for

yourself," I offered as soon as John hurried off. I'd planned to meet with Sasha to pick up Quinn with her, but Sasha had texted that she had a work errand near Quinn's school, so they planned to walk over together since it wasn't too far away.

My brother chuckled. "I will."

Moments later, we were seated in a conference room adjacent to Dallas's office, and I was wrestling with the urge to pull Sasha close. She looked worried, and I didn't like seeing her worried. Quinn, on the other hand, was annoyed.

She looked at Dallas, narrowing her eyes with her lips twisting slightly. "So basically, my father is a dumbass."

Dallas kept a straight face, although I saw the glint of laughter in his eyes. "If that's how you would like to define his choices, that's certainly your prerogative."

"Well, gambling is dumb and reckless. I mean, unless you have the money to back it up to begin with. I don't think it's a smart decision." Quinn looked toward Sasha and me as if seeking our agreement.

Sasha diplomatically shrugged. "Maybe."

I offered, "People are complicated."

Quinn rolled her eyes and looked back toward Dallas. "I brought my laptop," she offered. "Mom said you might want to look at it."

"I do if you don't mind," he replied.

"Since we forwarded the email to you, why do you want to see my laptop?" she asked as she pulled it out of her bag and slid it across the table to Dallas.

"Because I want to see source information and run a scan in your email to see if there are any other spam emails that link to that one."

Quinn nodded. "How long do you need it?"

"Not long. I can take it down to our tech guys, and then why don't we all go get lunch? Audrey is meeting me for lunch, and I thought we might as well all go together."

"That would be great," Sasha replied. "Audrey and I rarely manage to get together."

I'd been hoping to steal Sasha away for lunch at my place again, but then I suppose that wouldn't really work out with Quinn here.

"What time do you need to be back at school?" I asked, looking at Quinn as Dallas left the office to take the laptop to the tech forensics team.

"Mom took me out for the afternoon," Quinn said with a bright smile. "Can we go to the place where you got those yummy meat pies?"

"Absolutely."

Quinn's brow creased. "What if Audrey and Dallas want to go somewhere else?"

"I can vouch that Dallas loves that place too."

Quinn nodded before her gaze sobered quickly. "I wish my dad wasn't an idiot."

Sasha scooted her chair closer to Quinn. She curled her arm around her shoulders and gave her a quick side hug before pressing a kiss to her temple. "I'm sorry, honey. It sounds like he would like to be in touch. Would you like that?"

Quinn glanced at me. "What do you think?"

I almost countered with, "Me?" given how startled I was that she wanted my opinion, especially about an emotionally fraught topic such as this. I looked toward Sasha, trying to gauge if she wanted me to even answer. She nodded encouragingly.

I considered my words and my thoughts judiciously. "I think if your father wants to talk to you, you should consider how you'd feel if you decided not to. If it's something you think you'll regret, then give it a chance.

You don't have to do it alone. I know your mom will support you."

Quinn bit her bottom lip, tracing a circle with her fingertip over her denim-covered knee. "I'll have to think about it."

Chapter Twenty-Six

SASHA

Audrey walked down the sidewalk with me after we had lunch. Quinn was busy peppering Dallas and Noah with questions about the FBI, and they were both graciously answering them all.

"How are things with Noah?" Audrey asked.

I tucked my hands in my pockets, tipping my face up and enjoying the sun on this brisk winter day. "Good, I think. Things are moving a little fast."

"Is that a problem?" she asked when I glanced toward her.

"I'm not sure," I said slowly. "I've known him since we were kids, so I trust him. It's just, well, I've hardly dated. Being a single mom doesn't make it easy."

"I bet not," Audrey said gently. "For what it's worth, Dallas thinks Noah is in love with you. He says it makes perfect sense that he would fall for you."

"It does?" This startled me.

Audrey smiled when I slipped my gaze sideways as we walked shoulder to shoulder down the sidewalk. "Yes. Noah's a great babysitter, and I think the idea of family is really important to him. He's a little cynical, so falling for someone he already knew makes it easier for him to get past that. I saw him with you at the house at Christmas. It's obvious he's totally smitten. I'm not saying moving fast is always good, but it's not a given that it's a problem either. That's the way it happened for Dallas and me."

"Really?"

We stopped to wait for a light to change, and I glanced over my shoulder to see that Quinn, Noah, and Dallas were moving at a slower pace and still deep in conversation.

Audrey grinned. "Really. As you know, obviously Dallas and I knew each other too. We ended up at my parents' house unplanned over the holidays. When there's familiarity, I think you can kind of skip past a lot of the preliminaries." Her cheeks went a little pink. "We have more than enough chemistry, which seems to be the case for you and Noah," she teased lightly.

I laughed, feeling the heat rise in my cheeks. "Very true."

Our lunch companions caught up to us. When we began walking again, it felt natural that my hand slipped out of my pocket to find Noah's.

Chapter Twenty-Seven

SASHA

One month later

"What?!" I sputtered.

Melanie cast me a sly grin. "I'm just saying it is plain as day that man is in love with you."

"How do you know?" I pressed while my heart swooned hopefully.

I took a sip of my tea as Melanie gave me a warm look. "Dear, that man is there almost every night now. Technically, he's practically living there. He's embraced Quinn as if she's his own daughter, and she adores him. She's like a little sponge when he's around."

I felt a twinge in my heart. Not because I

didn't want Quinn to soak up Noah's affection like a sponge. I did, and it gave me so much joy that she was actually managing this adjustment. She still got cranky and snapped at me here and there, but it was regular teenage stuff. What stung a little in my heart was the awareness that, until now, she'd never had a father figure. I felt as if I'd somehow let her down. Even if I could talk myself out of that premise, it didn't change the fact my heart wanted to be able to give my daughter everything. That included waving a magic wand and re-creating her childhood so she had a father there the entire time. One thing that became painfully clear when you were a parent was just how much love could hurt on occasion.

I set my tea down and rested my chin in my palm. "I know she does. He's very good with her."

Melanie, because she was crazy perceptive and knew me well, cocked her head to the side. "Are you wishing you'd somehow been able to create a father out of whole cloth for her?"

I rolled my eyes. "Maybe," I said, realizing how ridiculous it was, even if it was the truth.

"You're an amazing mother, and Quinn

reflects that. You can't change the fact her biological father wasn't willing to step up."

"I know. Speaking of her biological father, Quinn did actually have a phone call with him. I still don't know how I feel about it. Honestly, we got so close to her being all grown up that I was kind of hoping I could just listen to her struggle to make her own decision if he ever reached out. Now, I feel like I need to manage it somehow."

"Hon," Melanie clucked. "Even if she was an adult, you would feel like you need to manage it. Trust me, I have two children, both of whom have been adults for many years, and both of whom I still worry about all the time. That's something most people don't fess up to. The worry doesn't end when they grow up." She cast me a rueful smile.

"I know. Funny thing, though. She wanted Noah there when she called her father."

"Did she say why?"

"She said that if anything weird happened, she'd have him right there. She does kind of love that Noah's an FBI agent. I don't think her father is a threat, although, apparently, he does have a bit of a gambling problem. Why do you think she wanted Noah there?"

"I think you're right, but also, he won't

have the kind of reaction you might if it didn't go well. Obviously, he cares about her. I don't mean to imply he doesn't. But you've been with her since before she was born. This is just *way* more for you emotionally as it is for her. Sometimes when something is really loaded, it's nice to have someone who is less deeply entwined in the issue there. If that makes any sense."

"That's pretty much what Noah thought," I said to her.

Her eyes twinkled. "I did tell you he was a smart man."

I laughed and took another sip of tea. "You did. It still feels like it's happening really fast."

"Maybe, maybe not. Look, I'm sure you can find some kind of self-help, or perhaps some research, telling you the right pace for a relationship. Anecdotally speaking, I don't think that's the question for you to answer. I've known people who took things slowly and divorced within a year of getting married. I've known people who took things slowly and were miserable the whole time and got married anyway and stayed married and miserable. On the other hand, I've known people who did things on a lark, and it worked out great. Life throws so many variables at us all the time. Add in another person, and there's another variable to deal with." She paused, her eyes measuring me. "I'd suggest that perhaps you keep pointing out it seems like it's going fast because that gives you something as an excuse and something to hang your fear on."

"I'm not afraid," I sputtered.

My old friend pursed her lips as she eyed me steadily.

"Oh, okay, fine. Maybe I am a little afraid. It's just it would break Quinn's heart if it didn't work out now."

"Quinn is very resilient," Melanie replied smoothly. "I don't think Noah is going to do anything reckless or stupid."

"Well, maybe he's being reckless by getting involved with me so quickly."

A low laugh rustled in Melanie's throat. "Perhaps, but I don't think so."

There was a light knock on Melanie's door, and we both glanced over to see it swinging open. Quinn poked her head around the door. "Mom, can I make some popcorn?"

I glanced at my watch and back at her. "Sure, but it's an hour before bedtime."

"I know." She blew a kiss to Melanie and then disappeared, calling, "Thanks, Mom!" just as the door closed behind her.

"I should get back to our place. Always good to visit," I said as I stood from the table.

I crossed over to the sink to rinse my mug and set it in the dishwasher. That was the kind of neighbors we were with Melanie. She would do the same in our place. She followed me to the door. "I'll miss having you as a neighbor."

"What?" I had just started to turn the doorknob, and my hand froze as I looked back toward her.

She winked. "I hope you'll actually move in with Noah at some point. And Lord knows, you deserve some more space."

My chest pinched with worry. "What will —?" I began.

Melanie shook her head. "Don't you dare use some sort of flimsy excuse that you need to stay my neighbor to prevent you from moving forward with Noah. Yes, you and Quinn have been my neighbors for over a decade, and I consider you family. You're not going to lose me. I'll finally be able to raise the rent. There, that'll give you a reason to go."

"Melanie, you can raise the rent. I can afford it."

"I'm teasing, plus it's my call." She pulled

me into a quick hug and then pretty much shoved me out the door.

As I crossed the hall, my eyes were drawn down to the front entrance when I heard the door opening. The second I saw Noah coming in, my heart let out a cheer. Seeing him made my entire body smile if that was possible.

I waited, my hand resting on the smooth railing on top of the stairs. As soon as he saw me, he pocketed his keys and came up the stairs two at a time. He stopped in front of me, and I was breathless merely at his presence.

I smiled up at him. "Hey. I didn't know you were coming tonight."

"I texted over an hour ago, but you didn't reply, so I got worried."

A little thrill ran through me. It was silly, but it was nice to have somebody worry about me. "I left my phone in my apartment. I was having tea with Melanie," I explained.

He stepped closer, sliding an arm around my waist as he pressed a kiss to my temple and then my mouth. The moment his lips brushed over mine, our kiss went from a brief greeting to deep and searching. Only Noah could do that to me. Undiluted pleasure raced through me, and I moaned in his mouth.

The sound of the door opening behind us nudged my awareness. Noah lifted his head, and I was breathless.

"Hi, Noah," Melanie said in a deceptively level voice. "Just checking my mail," she added as she walked down the stairs in her robe.

"Hey there, Melanie," Noah called. "Always good to see you."

"Likewise!" she returned.

I bit my lip to keep from giggling as he stepped away, his hand sliding down my back and coaxing me forward. A moment later, we were in my apartment, and I finally let my laughter loose as I leaned against the door.

"What's so funny?" Quinn asked when she glanced over at us from the kitchen.

My cheeks got even hotter. Noah's smile was bland as he glanced over and shrugged out of his jacket. "Is that popcorn I smell?" he asked, deftly ignoring her question.

Quinn nodded. "Want some?"

"Maybe. Is it the kettle kind?"

He finished taking off his shoes and walked into the kitchen as I trailed behind him a little more slowly, thinking that we had more than enough chaperones around between my daughter and our elderly neighbor.

"Of course," Quinn replied. They had already established that they shared the same preference for popcorn.

"Should we make a second one?" Noah asked solemnly as he rested his shoulder on the inside of the archway between the living room and kitchen.

Quinn shook her head. "Don't think so. I don't want the whole bag. Are you going to want some, Mom?" Her eyes bounced to mine.

I felt stuck where I was, absorbing their easy interaction and realizing that maybe this moment felt mundane but also huge. Nothing was remarkable about it. Just my teenage daughter sharing popcorn with my boyfriend, the very first boyfriend I'd ever officially had since high school. It felt like a family, and there was a peculiar ache in my heart, a desire so fierce I was almost afraid to let myself actually want it.

"Mom?" Quinn prompted.

Giving my head a little shake, I replied, "No. Do you want to watch something together?"

I guessed Quinn was going to turn us down, but lately, she'd surprised me. "Can we watch that nature show, the one where they travel all over?" she prompted.

I nodded. Noah was crossing through the kitchen to open the refrigerator—because, yeah, we were at that stage. I turned away to turn on the television, swallowing through the emotion thickening in my throat. These were good tears, but I wasn't in the mood to cry in front of Noah and Quinn because then I'd have to explain.

A few minutes later, the three of us and Matilda were on the couch. Matilda was happily curled up beside Quinn. She liked to stretch out between Quinn and the end of the couch, pressing her nose into the cushions.

Noah's arm was curled around my shoulders, and a bowl of popcorn sat on the couch between him and Quinn. Everything felt just right, comfortable. I was almost afraid to think this could be more than this. Because what if that broke the spell?

Chapter Twenty-Eight

NOAH

"We really need to get some furniture here," Sasha commented as she surveyed the only bedroom with a bed in it at my family's home in Haven's Bay.

I caught her hand in mine and reeled her to me, where I sat on the foot of the bed. I rested my hands on her hips and couldn't resist letting one slide down over the sweet curve of her bottom. I gave it a squeeze and watched as pink crested on her cheeks.

"I think a bed is plenty. That's all we need," I said, endeavoring to keep a straight face.

Sasha bit her bottom lip as she stared at me, her eyes close to level with mine, where she stood caged between my knees. "I suppose. Good thing we have a couch and a TV too. But I'd like to bring Quinn up here. She's asked to come, and we don't have a bed for her."

"Good point," I said, lightly bumping my forehead against her breastbone. "Let's bring her up soon, and she can pick out a bed for one of the bedrooms."

"She'd love that."

"How come you didn't tell me she wanted to come?"

As much as I wanted a weekend with Sasha all to myself, Quinn was awesome to have around. It was important for me to spend time with her, and I knew it meant everything to Sasha.

"I told you now. She didn't ask to come this weekend," Sasha assured me. "She's happy to spend the weekend with her aunt. She just said someday she'd like to come, and I don't want to put her on an air mattress. I know she'd survive, but maybe you guys would eventually like to furnish this place." Her voice lilted up at the end.

"Next time then," I promised.

She sifted her fingers through my hair, sending a fiery sizzle down my spine. Her hand slid to curl around the back of my neck. She dipped her head, nipping lightly on the side of my neck before pressing hot, open-mouthed kisses along the underside of my jaw.

Lust rolled through me. I experienced a sweet, fiery shock of pleasure when her lips captured mine. I kept thinking I would get used to it, that my body's unrestrained reaction to her would begin to temper like glass to withstand the heat. It wasn't happening.

Our kiss went wild as I slid my hand down to cup her bottom and bring her flush against me. I could feel the tight peaks of her nipples pressing through her shirt. Needing air, I broke free, almost roughly, burying my forehead against her chest as I gulped in air.

"Fuck. You drive me crazy, Sasha." My words were muffled against her.

Lifting my head, I found her gaze waiting. Her pupils were dilated, and her eyes dark with need. Her breath was coming in tattered gasps. I lifted my hand, trailing my knuckles lightly over the side of her neck, feeling the wild thrum of her pulse.

"Kiss me," she ordered.

"My pleasure." My words formed against her lips as I closed the incremental distance between us when I spoke.

Everything around us felt electrified, the

very air itself heating as if our desire was fire and every touch oxygen to fan the flames.

Somehow, everything always felt rushed with her. My need was too great, and I couldn't slow the rush of its force. Our clothes came off in a rush, left scattered on the floor at the foot of the bed. Just the week before, Sasha had pointed out she was on birth control. I knew for her it was a big deal to place her trust in me on that score, so it had taken some convincing from her that we could pass on continuing to use condoms.

I swallowed as I looked up at her when she straddled me. I felt the slick kiss of the very core of her. Then the slow, clenching slide when she sheathed me. I watched her, my own pleasure tightening at the base of my spine. Her cheeks were flushed, her skin dewy, and her soft plush curves pressed close to me. Every rock of her hips drove me closer and closer to release.

I clung to the frayed thread of my control, waiting until I felt her body begin to tremble. Reaching between us, I teased my fingers over her swollen, slippery clit. She cried out, her pussy clamping down around my cock. I finally let loose, my release slamming through me.

By the time I could breathe and my

thoughts flickered back online, I felt as if I'd been cast ashore by a rough wave that left me disoriented. Pleasure echoed through me in lazy ripples.

Sasha's head was tucked against my shoulder, and I sifted my fingers through her hair. My heart knew the truth. I loved her. The peace I felt whenever we were together like this was so profound I felt it to my bones.

I finally gave voice to those feelings. "I love you."

Sasha had relaxed against me, a bundle of curves. In a mere second, I felt her tension. She held still and then lifted her head, her eyes searching mine, doubts passing through hers like clouds on a sunny day.

"Noah—" she began.

"I don't expect you to say it back. I just wanted to let you know how I felt. Because it matters."

She blinked, and her eyes were bright. A tear slipped off her lashes, and I brushed it away. "Well, now," I whispered. "That wasn't supposed to make you cry."

She blinked again, another tear rolling down, which I captured with my thumb. "It's not that. You just startled me." She took a quick breath. "I love you too."

My chest felt filled with lightness as if all

the doors to my heart were flung open and fresh air was rushing through. I tipped my head forward, my forehead coming to rest against hers.

"Okay, then," I whispered.

Chapter Twenty-Nine

SASHA

Another month later

"What do you mean?" I asked.

Noah was making coffee. He hadn't moved in, although sometimes it felt like he might as well. Quinn wasn't up yet because it was Saturday.

He hit the start button and turned, resting his hips against the counter and curling his hands over the edge as he looked at me from across the kitchen where I sat at the table. "I mean, I told him to back off."

A flash of defensiveness rose inside, irritation stampeding behind it. We were talking about Quinn's father. Over the past month,

Quinn had had a few phone calls with him and actually met him once with me and Noah present.

About a week ago, Quinn had shared that she was comfortable with occasional contact, but she didn't want anything beyond that. Now, come to find out, Noah had taken it upon himself to intervene.

If I had a button, this was it—anything and everything connected to Quinn's biological father. Every decision I tried to make around him felt fraught and tangled. I felt like I was walking on a tightrope, not even sure if it was better to try to keep my balance or allow myself to fall and hope my landing would be cushioned.

Hot tears stung my eyes, and I blinked them back, feeling my cheeks flush hot and then cold. "Noah, why would you do that?"

"Sasha, I thought Quinn said—"

"Quinn said what?"

It was obvious when Noah picked up that I was upset. His eyes searched my face. "That she didn't want it to be more than the occasional phone call to check-in."

"But why would you say something to him? Did he call you?"

I crossed my arms tightly in front of my chest as I waited.

"He did. That's why I'm telling you this. Because he called me."

"But why would he call you instead of me? And why didn't you tell me?"

"I'm telling you now." Noah crossed over to where I had stood from the table in my agitation.

"You could've told me last night," I protested.

"Sasha, you were in bed when I got here last night. I had a late night at work."

Logically, I knew what he said to be true. He had texted me that they had a break on a case and were doing interviews. He'd climbed in bed beside me and pulled me close. I had a hazy memory of waking during the night with him spooned behind me and the press of his arousal against my bottom. We made sleepy love in the dark, and I'd fallen back asleep, thinking things were good, *really* good.

And now this. I swallowed, trying to batten down my annoyance. I hated the look in his eyes. I sensed he was picking up that I was spiraling a little bit.

"I don't know why he called me instead of you. All I did was reiterate what I knew Quinn already told him."

I took a quick breath. "Okay. Next time he calls you, please tell him to call me."

"I did. I just hadn't gotten to that part yet."

Right then, the sound of Quinn's bedroom door opening came from the hallway. I sat down at the table again, swallowing and looking down at the crossword puzzle I'd been doing. Noah had enough sense to know that I didn't want to discuss this further, not with Quinn around.

I didn't want to discuss it further at all. If I could've, I wanted to rewind the morning and go so far back that Quinn's father would know he had to call me, not to call my boyfriend, who was feeling more and more a part of my family.

What I hadn't told Noah yet was how Quinn said that Noah felt like more of a father to her than her actual biological father. Those were big feelings for her, and I didn't know what was going to happen long term. A part of me was thrilled for Quinn to accept him on this level, yet it felt like I was losing something with her. Between her biological father being in touch with us and Noah interwoven into our daily lives, the tight bond I'd shared with her was changing.

"Morning," Quinn called in a sing-song voice as she entered the kitchen.

I lifted my head, replying, "Morning." I thought my voice sounded normal.

Noah set a cup of coffee in front of me. I was grateful because a few swallows loosened the aching knot of emotion in my throat.

"Thanks for making oatmeal," Quinn said to Noah.

That was another thing. He always made her oatmeal now. I was feeling crazy this morning because just the other morning, I'd been so grateful for everything he did. They both liked oatmeal for breakfast. Mornings were always a scramble. Noah usually got up a little earlier than me and was showering before I even rolled out of bed.

I was feeling restless in my skin. I wanted to shake off my frustration. I knew I wasn't being logical, which only added to my annoyance. A little while later, he kissed me on the cheek and left while Quinn finished her oatmeal.

As if I was on some kind of mission to ruin my morning, a few minutes later, I stumbled into another maddening conversation with my daughter, and it was entirely my fault. "Apparently, your father called Noah."

Quinn lifted her head as she took the last bite of her oatmeal, watching me and waiting.

"I asked Noah to make sure he called me instead of him if anything came up," I added.

She set her spoon down. The sound of it clicking against the edge of the bowl echoed in our small kitchen. "Why?" She blinked at me behind her glasses.

"Because I'm your mother," I finally said, struck by her question but uncertain the meaning of it was as emotionally loaded as I interpreted it.

She blinked again. "I don't mind if he calls Noah."

"Do you have a problem if he calls me? Last I checked, you're not eighteen yet."

"Geez, Mom, why are you so upset about it? Noah's here all the time. I like him. And frankly, if my dad's going to be a dick, it's probably better if Noah deals with it. He's not gonna fuck with Noah."

"He's not gonna fuck with me," I countered, completely ignoring her choice of language and using it myself. Yay, welcome to the great mom show.

As if she could read my freaking mind, Quinn returned with, "Nice language, Mom. Why are you so upset?"

"I'm not upset," I lied. "I just think it's

best if your father has a question about you that he calls me."

Because teenagers were crazy perceptive at all the wrong times, Quinn asked, "Why are you acting like a dog pissing on a tree?"

"What?" I countered, ignoring the rising tide of defensiveness that threatened to pull me under.

"In this case, I am the tree. Or rather any decisions about my father are the tree," she added.

"Quinn, I—" I sputtered. I managed a breath and grasped onto the thin thread of my composure. "Ugh."

"Right." Her eyes narrowed as she smirked. "Noah is here all the time, and I know you want me to be okay with him being a part of our family. Well, he's involved, and I don't mind my dad calling him."

I kept my cool, but just barely. I didn't really know why I was freaking out. I nodded and stood to go take a shower.

Just when I thought that shitty conversation was over, Quinn had to needle me a little bit more. I hurried through a shower and yanked on my work clothes. When I returned to the kitchen, I noticed she had left her bowl out. At that moment, she came down the hallway swinging her backpack over her shoulder. "Please clean up," I said, my tone sharp.

Her bag fell to the floor with a loud thump in the middle of the living room. "Fine. You can't have it both ways, you know?" she snapped as she crossed the kitchen to grab her bowl. She rinsed it in the sink and put it in the dishwasher, closing it loudly.

"What are you talking about?"

"Trying to be all tough around boundaries with both my dad and Noah, and trying to be in charge of everything. You can't ask me to be open and accepting about Noah, and then be a bitch about it later."

I realized how much I'd screwed up when I saw tears in her eyes. She didn't give me a chance when I began, "Sweetie—"

"Save it." She dashed past me, the door slamming behind her as she hurried away.

The tears that had been threatening all morning spilled over. I leaned my hips against the counter and cried.

Chapter Thirty

NOAH

"What the fuck?" I muttered to myself. I stared down at my phone after I finished playing Sasha's message.

Just then, Dallas appeared in the doorway to my office. His eyes arced around the room, a crease forming between his brows when he looked back at me. "Who were you talking to?"

"My phone," I said, holding it up.

"What's up?" He walked in quickly, stopping in front of my desk.

"Sasha just left me a message and said we needed to take a break."

"Out of nowhere?"

I nodded slowly.

"Did something happen?" he prompted.

I leaned back in my chair, restlessly drumming my fingertips on the armrest. "I think so. Remember how I mentioned Quinn's dad called yesterday?"

Dallas nodded briskly. "Yeah, and you said you were going to tell Sasha."

"I did, and she got upset. I didn't think it was *this* kind of upset."

"You should probably talk to her."

Galvanized, I stood from my desk. I didn't know why Sasha was so upset, but I wasn't going to sit on this. Roughly a half an hour later, I was at her apartment. She was maintaining a cool silence.

In contrast, Quinn had things to say. "So Mom has an opinion."

"What's that?" I countered lightly, wishing I had reconsidered my plan to come over. We didn't need an audience for this conversation.

"I guess my dad's not supposed to call you about anything to do with me. Only she's in charge of that. You know, boundaries and stuff." Quinn's tone was snide, and I wanted to tell her to cut it out. But now definitely wasn't the time.

Sasha's shoulders were held in a tense line as she stood at the kitchen counter, emptying the dishwasher. "Quinn, do you mind if I talk to your mom privately?"

That seemed to give her pause as her eyes bounced uncertainly from me to her mother and back again. "Why?"

"Because I would like to speak to your mother privately," I explained the obvious.

"If it's about me, I should be here." Quinn twisted her lips with a little smirk.

Quinn generally wasn't that annoying as a teenager. She had her moments, but this one was definitely the most frustrating of my experience.

"It's not about you." Which was true. I'd mishandled the situation, and Quinn's involvement in it was secondary.

Quinn eyed me suspiciously, but she finally shrugged. "Fine." She flounced out of the kitchen and down the hallway. I waited until I heard her door shut.

"Sasha—" I began.

"Now really isn't a good time. Trust me, she can hear us from her bedroom."

"Can I at least apologize?"

Sasha turned to face me, finally looking me in the eye for more than a passing glance. Her gaze was shuttered. Everything about her screamed that she had her walls firmly in place.

"I overstepped. I shouldn't have even talked to her dad. I should've just called you and told you."

She blinked at me. She and Quinn shared that habit, blinking when they were thinking hard. My heart twisted in my chest. I was in love with Sasha, and I also loved Quinn. In mere months, the two of them felt indispensable in my life. I would do anything to make sure they were okay, to keep them safe.

"What is it?" I heard myself asking, pressing ahead even though I probably shouldn't.

"I appreciate your apology, but I need some time."

I heard Quinn's door opening, followed by the bathroom door closing a few seconds later. "Can we have lunch together tomorrow?" I asked, keeping my voice low.

"I'll call you."

"Sasha, please."

"I'll call you," she repeated.

Because she seemed to have a sixth sense, Quinn came out of the bathroom and back into the kitchen. This girl, who spent most evenings in her bedroom unless prodded by us, plopped down at the kitchen table with her laptop. "Mom, I need some help with math," she announced.

I opened my mouth to offer to help. Because Sasha hated math. I didn't mind math. Not that I thought I was better at it, but I had, in fact, helped Quinn with her math homework several times.

When I looked at Sasha, she simply shook her head, just barely.

Quinn looked at me. "I think that means you're supposed to leave. She overreacts like this sometimes."

Sasha's expression turned stony. I wanted, badly, to cross the kitchen and pull her into my arms and melt her anger away. I didn't want to leave, but I wasn't going to make a scene in front of Quinn, so I said, "I'll call you tomorrow."

For the first time in months, I didn't spend the night with Sasha curled up warm beside me, her silky skin pressed against mine.

Hours later, I lay in my own bed, missing Sasha acutely and feeling frustrated. I punched my pillows because I couldn't get them right. Restless, I reached for my phone and typed out a quick text to her.

Me: *To reiterate, I'm sorry. I'm not exactly sure how I screwed up so badly, but please talk to me.*

Sasha: *I'll call when I'm ready.*

Chapter Thirty-One

SASHA

"Drama much?" Melanie asked.

My mouth dropped open. "Drama?"

She nodded, pursing her lips before taking a sip of coffee.

It was a full week later, and I still hadn't called Noah. He tried to call me and texted and sent me flowers twice—at work and here. Melanie had answered the door for that delivery, so she knew I'd gotten them. She'd even read the card.

"Yes," she repeated after she swallowed her coffee and straightened in her chair. "You're overreacting. Now that you've overreacted, you're compounding it. I know you well enough to say that, and you need to hear it."

I opened my mouth to protest, but she held her hand up. "Wait. You know I love you and Quinn like family. You have been raising her by yourself since you had her. It makes complete sense that you're overprotective. You've had to be. It's always been just you. I never dated as a single mother, but I can imagine it's like walking through a field of landmines. There's no easy way to do it. It's a constant dance of who to let in, how to keep your distance, and how to assess when to let someone into your life and get to know your daughter."

Tears stung in my eyes, but I nodded, the defensiveness inside easing slightly. "It is. Noah's the first man I introduced to Quinn."

"Of course. He's a keeper."

"I don't know why I'm reacting like this," I finally mumbled, feeling a little ridiculous about it all.

I was missing Noah so fiercely that it annoyed me. I fell asleep crying twice this week. I knew my pride was getting in the way, but I didn't know what to do next.

"I think two things are happening. Quinn's father showing up in the midst of that investigation is stressful. Trying to trust him is huge. He seems, at best, marginally interested in connecting with her," Melanie said, her tone soft.

"I know. He's been nice, and I think he does want to connect, but he doesn't grasp that she's a teenager and has her own feelings and opinions."

"Teenagers are not easy, even for those of us who know what to do with them. There's that, which would definitely bring up all kinds of stuff for you, and then letting Noah in, and *really* letting him in. Quinn loves him, and it's obvious to me she looks at him like a father figure. I'm sure you love that, but it's also hard because it's just been you and her against the world. I like to think I'm part of your family, but it's not the same."

"You are," I broke in.

She smiled warmly. "Good. But I'm off to the side. I'm not there day in and day out and never will be. If you and Noah stay together, he'll be more than just someone on the side, and I think that scares you. I can't speak for him, but my gut tells me he's in it all the way."

I swiped at my tears and gulped my coffee. After a moment, I asked, "So I should probably call him?" I looked down at my coffee cup as if that would tell me what to do.

"Or at least answer when he calls," she

said. "Before you call him, I think you should talk to Quinn. She's being a little shitty about this."

"What do you mean?"

Melanie drummed her fingertips on the table before replying, "She's angry with you for setting a limit about something that's your prerogative. Teenagers have that tendency."

My chest felt tight, and my throat was a little scratchy. I knew precisely what Melanie meant, and while I knew she was right, this was one topic I didn't want to press my daughter on. It was the kind of sore spot that felt so vulnerable, as if torn open, the wound might deepen.

"I'll think about it," I finally said.

Chapter Thirty-Two

NOAH

I glared at my sister. "What do you mean?"

"I mean, maybe you need to do something other than burying yourself in work," Thea said.

"Thea, Sasha told me to give her space. Now you're telling me to ignore that?"

My sister pursed her lips, giving me a pointed look. "Not ignore it, but perhaps make it clear how you feel."

I threw my hands up in the air as I turned, walking across my living room to look out the front windows. It was evening in Boston, and rush-hour traffic could be heard in the distance. I watched the cars passing by below. Stuffing my hands in my pockets, I turned. The echo of my footsteps on the floor annoyed me. The space felt empty. I'd become accustomed to staying at Sasha's. Although her apartment was small, the two most important people in my world were there—Sasha and Quinn.

When I met my sister's eyes from across the room where she stood by the couch, her gaze softened, and her lips twisted to the side. "You look sad. You really love her, don't you?"

My chest was uncomfortably tight, balled with emotion. Looking down, I dragged the toe of my shoe across one of the flooring planks as I nodded. "Yeah, I do." I shrugged when I looked at Thea again. "And she won't have me."

Thea shook her head. "She will." She let out a short sigh followed by a low laugh. "I can't believe Dallas, and now you have both fallen for my friends. It seems convenient, but also annoying."

"Well, it could be awkward if Sasha and I don't work this out."

"Send her flowers."

"Again?"

Thea nodded firmly. "Yes. She's been living the non glamorous life of a single mom. She's never been wooed. You two fell together quickly. So woo her. I don't think it'll take much. Whether it's flowers or something else, do something to woo her."

I was game. I would try just about anything to win Sasha back. I felt as if I were walking a tightrope. I wanted to respect her feelings but make sure she knew how much I cared. I stared back at my sister. I knew just the thing.

Chapter Thirty-Three

SASHA

A light knock sounded on the apartment door before it opened. Glancing over, I smiled when I saw Melanie peering inside. "Hey there, come on in." I gestured for her to step into the living room. I was in the kitchen emptying the dishwasher.

I'd had a long few days at work because my boss was dealing with a complicated case. We'd been preparing reams of documents for the court hearing.

"I would, but I'm headed out to my daughter's house for dinner," Melanie replied. "Someone's downstairs for you with a delivery."

"Oh?"

Melanie's eyes twinkled with her smile. "Yes."

I put away the two plates I had just set on the counter and turned. I followed her out of my apartment and closed the door before jogging downstairs. "Enjoy dinner," I called as she walked out the door and passed the deliveryman waiting under the porch light.

"Hello?" I said, uncertainly.

"Hi there," he said easily. He handed over a large paper bag. "Dinner," he explained at my look of confusion.

"I didn't order dinner."

He shrugged. "You're Sasha, apartment two?" At my nod, he added, "Well, somebody ordered it for you. Enjoy."

Bemused, I accepted the bag and fished in my pocket, abruptly realizing I didn't have my wallet to tip him. "I'm sorry. Let me go upstairs and get my wallet."

He shook his head, flashing a grin. "I've already been tipped." With a wink and a wave, he jogged off the porch.

I walked up the stairs. I didn't know why, but I waited until I was in my apartment to open the bag. Quinn was in her bedroom, working on homework.

Crossing into the kitchen after I kicked off my shoes, I opened it. It was then I noticed the distinctive label of the English pub where Noah had taken us for dinner, and then Quinn several times after that because she loved it so.

There was a note tucked inside. When I unfolded it, tears welled and splashed on my cheeks.

Consider this a peace offering. I miss you, and I love you. Noah

The scroll was bold and clear. A full week had passed since Melanie had encouraged me to talk to him. I hadn't.

As bad luck would have it, I heard Quinn's bedroom door opening. I swiped at my tears, but she appeared just as I reached for a napkin to blow my nose.

She stopped by the kitchen table, and I stared at her bright pink socks. They were her favorite kind, fuzzy and soft. The very kind of socks she loved when she was a little girl, and I still got them for her. That detail brought a fresh wave of tears. I blinked, wishing I wasn't falling apart in front of my daughter.

"What's wrong, Mom?"

"Noah sent us dinner."

Quinn peered into the bag, but she didn't smile. Her worried eyes searched my face. "Why are you crying?"

"I miss Noah." My honest answer slipped out before I could stop it.

Quinn sat across from me at the table, pushing her glasses up on her nose as she blinked at me solemnly. "Well, I think you should tell him."

The wisdom of a teenager. And she was right. "I'm going to."

"Call him now." She stood, striding over to the counter where my phone sat by the refrigerator.

She set it on the table in front of me as she sat down again. "Text him and tell him to come over."

"Quinn, it's not that simple. And I don't feel like making up with him in front of you," I said, shaking my head slightly, amused despite the emotion clogging my throat and making my heart ache.

"I'll go to my room and put my headphones on," she offered so earnestly my heart twisted a little.

I took a breath, thinking maybe that would work.

"I'm sorry," she said suddenly. "I know you didn't understand when I wanted to talk to Noah about my dad. I didn't mean to hurt your feelings."

Those pesky tears spilled over, the force

of them too much for me to blink back. "You don't need to apologize, sweetie. I want you to feel like you can talk to Noah, or Melanie, or any adult you trust. I know I have baggage around your dad, and sometimes it gets in the way."

My little girl, who was getting all grown up faster than I wanted, nodded sagely.

More tears splashed onto my cheeks. Not for this moment, but for the twists and turns on the road that brought me here. That was the sharp twist of love. I was so proud to have a daughter who could care and understand this much. It meant she was growing up, and I would have to let go of my little girl a piece at a time.

After we hugged, she took her sandwich out of the paper bag, filled a glass of water, and pointed at my phone. "Call Noah. I'll be in my room, and I promise I won't listen."

———

I didn't wait. The second I heard her door close, I lifted my phone and pulled up Noah's phone number. He answered on the second ring. As soon as I heard his voice, I couldn't think of what to say. My feelings were spinning inside each other and bouncing around in my brain. My breath was locked in my lungs, and I was silent.

"Sasha?" Noah prompted into the quiet line.

The sound of his voice seemed to set me free. Tears were rolling down my cheeks, and I was relieved he couldn't see what a mess I was. "It's me," I finally said between sniffles.

"Are you okay?" His tone was even, but I could sense a touch of alarm.

I sniffled again, finally grabbing a napkin on the table and wiping it across my eyes. "I'm fine. Thank you for the dinner."

"You're welcome."

We fell quiet again, and I tried to think of what to say. My mouth was ahead of my brain. "I love you."

"I love you too."

"I kind of panicked. Everything around Quinn is sort of a button for me."

"I understand. I didn't think through what it might feel like for you."

"You shouldn't have to," I insisted.

"No, I should. Things felt good with us, but I didn't think about how this was different. You've been raising Quinn all by yourself since she was a baby. I overstepped."

"I appreciate that, but I also overreacted.

Can we call it a draw, and you come over tonight?"

"Absolutely. When should I be there?"

"Now would be good," I replied, feeling bashful.

"Be there in ten."

"Wait!"

"What is it?"

"You only sent two sandwiches. I don't want you to be hungry."

"I'll pick one up on the way over. Wait for me before you eat."

As soon as I hung up, I heard the sound of Quinn's bedroom door opening and rolled my eyes. Of course she'd been listening. Maybe I should've been embarrassed, but I was too filled with a rushing sense of joy mingled with peace to worry over it.

"You told him to come over, right?" Quinn asked when she appeared at the end of the hallway.

I swiped my tears away and nodded. "Do you want to eat with us?"

Her smile was slow and sweet. "I'll eat in my room. Let's watch a show afterward. You need a little bit of privacy." She spun away, waving over her shoulder as she hurried down the hallway. "But for God's sake, don't go crazy in the kitchen," she called right before she closed her door.

My cheeks were still hot when Noah arrived a few minutes later. When he wrapped me in his arms, I breathed him in, thanking the universe and the stars that I hadn't screwed this up too badly.

By the time he drew back, joy and need were spinning through me. "Quinn said we couldn't go too crazy in the kitchen," I said breathlessly.

Noah chuckled. "Smart girl. Now let's eat."

We sat at the kitchen table and ate together. I savored every second of the quiet simplicity of the moments. When Quinn came out of her bedroom to join us to watch a show, I was curled up against Noah's side with his arm around my shoulders and Matilda napping at our feet.

EPILOGUE

Noah

Christmas Eve — the following winter

I reflexively checked my coat pocket. For perhaps the fiftieth time in the past hour, I confirmed it was still there.

"Do you have it?" Quinn whispered, loud enough that the very whisper itself echoed in the foyer.

I cast a warning look, albeit a bemused one, at Sasha's daughter. "Yes, I have it."

"I'll be right there!" Sasha's voice carried to us from the hallway upstairs.

Quinn tapped the toe of her chunky black leather boot on the floor. "You know," she said as her eyes arced around the foyer and down the hallway, "you need to step it up on furnishing this place."

I chuckled, arching a brow as I looked back at her. "You don't say?"

Quinn, who looked so much like Sasha it was startling sometimes, nodded as she pushed her glasses up her nose. "Yes. You don't have anything other than a coat rack in here. You need like a table and maybe a rug or something. This could be a room itself. I'm just grateful you got a bed for the guest room."

I grinned. "You know, we don't live here," I pointed out.

Since last Christmas, Sasha and I had actually come up here for a few weekends. Suffice it to say, we didn't use that time to furnish the house. We had other things to do. Sasha had pointed out that dating a single mother wasn't glamorous, which turned out to be true, but dating anyone who had a life wasn't glamorous. Occasional weekend getaways gave us a little freedom. Quinn was an awesome kid—the best, as far as I was concerned.

"How about we go to that furniture store in the next town over? Pretty sure they'll be closed for Christmas Day, but they'll probably be open the day after."

Quinn's eyes lit up. "Ooh, that'll be fun."

A flash of trepidation stole through me. Quinn liked things bright, and I didn't know if my siblings, who technically had a say since we jointly owned the house, would have an opinion on that. I dismissed the concern quickly. They'd all welcomed Quinn into our family, and honestly, most of us could only make it to this house periodically.

At the sound of footsteps, I glanced up to see Sasha descending the stairs, and my breath seized in my lungs for a moment. She always looked gorgeous, but tonight my anticipation had me on edge. Everything felt sharper, including how beautiful she was. Her hair was down, which was rare. Sasha was a practical woman, and I loved that, but it was nice to see her hair loose on occasion.

She wore fitted jeans with low-heeled leather boots paired with a cream silk blouse and a bright blue silk scarf. Her lips were shiny, and I wanted to kiss that lip gloss right off.

I knew any PDA would lead to Quinn snorting. So I made do with sliding my arm around Sasha's waist when she stopped beside us. "Are we ready?" she asked.

"*We've* been ready," Quinn said with a sly grin.

Sasha didn't even bother reacting to Quinn's comment. She was a master at not engaging. All things considered, Quinn only occasionally gave us too much attitude.

Sasha turned and snagged her coat off the coat rack by the door. As we walked out into the crisp winter air on Christmas Eve, Quinn commented, "Noah's going to let me start furnishing this place."

Sasha's eyes widened when she glanced at me while we descended the front steps.

"We *do* need some more furniture. We'll see what we can find," I said easily.

We drove into downtown Haven's Bay. Our small hometown was spruced up for the holidays. There were wreaths mounted on the streetlights and holiday lights glittering on the big tree in the town green beside Main Street. Most of the homes and stores had lights strung along the rooftops.

I smiled to myself, recalling our Christmas tree shopping venture just the night before. We'd let Quinn pick, and she decided we needed to take the most forlorn-looking tree. "To make it feel better about itself," she'd said.

A few minutes later, we sat in the parking lot at Emile's. "Now," Sasha said as she looked over her shoulder at Quinn. "We'll be back before nine o'clock. You'd better be here."

Quinn let out a put-upon sigh. "Of course, I'll be here. You know the people who own this place. I'm sure they'll text you if I leave."

We were dropping her off at a small holiday gathering organized by the town's theater group. Quinn had gotten involved with her high school theater program in Boston and made a few friends through a regional traveling theater program. One of those friends happened to be from Haven's Bay.

"I know," Sasha said, her lips pressing in a line. "We'll go have dinner and be back later. Have fun."

Quinn leaned forward and kissed her mother on the cheek before climbing out of the car and jogging across the parking lot. She waved, and the sound of the holiday sleigh bells on the door jingled as she disappeared through it.

"Let's go have dinner." I backed up and rolled slowly out of the parking lot.

"Am I too overprotective?" Sasha asked as I drove the short distance to Bay Bistro.

I shrugged. "I don't know that any parent can feel too overprotective. I think all you can do is try to find a balance. It's the best you can hope for."

A short while later, Sherry was beaming at us as she filled our wine glasses. "Should I leave the bottle?" she asked.

"Just a glass for me. I'm driving. Do you think you can finish that bottle yourself?" I teased with a glance at Sasha.

Sasha rolled her eyes. "No. Just one glass is good for me too."

After we ordered our food, my heart was thudding rapidly, the sound of it echoing in my ears. I'd told myself to wait until dessert, but I was too restless to relax.

I made a quick decision, sliding my hand into my pocket. The small velvet box warmed as I held it loosely in my palm under the table.

"Sasha?"

Her lashes swung up, and she held my gaze. I usually managed to have some eloquence, but I couldn't seem to do this any way other than bluntly. "Will you marry me?"

Sasha's mouth fell open in a pretty O, and her eyes went wide. "What?"

This time, I remembered to bring the ring out from under the table and open the small box.

SASHA

I stared at the ring—a simple platinum band with a row of sapphires along one edge. That alone had tears stinging my eyes. Because he remembered that Quinn worried about conflict diamonds, and as a result, so did I. Because when you were a mom, it was an endless experience of vicarious worry.

I swallowed, trying to calm the emotion threatening to catch me in a riptide as it rushed through me. "What?" I repeated.

Noah's eyes held mine, his gaze steady and sure. "Will you marry me?"

I pressed my palm to my chest, almost fearful my heart might beat its way out. "Are you serious?"

"I'm so serious I even asked Quinn about it," he said somberly.

I gasped. "Oh, my God. Yes! Of course, yes!"

I wasn't really paying attention to what I was doing and almost knocked my wine over when I moved from my chair and all but threw myself into his lap.

Noah, because he was that kind of guy, reached over to steady the wobbling wineglass with one hand as he wrapped his other arm around my waist and held me close.

"For a second there," he murmured, his lips near my ear and sending a hot shiver through me, "I thought you might say no."

I lifted my head, immediately ensnared in his ebullient gaze. "Not a chance."

He slipped the ring on my finger. Just then, Sherry appeared by our table again, a smile on her face and her eyes absolutely beaming with joy. "Is this what I think it is?"

I lifted my hand, and she inspected the ring, oohing and aahing and then offering us a bottle of champagne.

"We'd love the champagne, but can we take it home?" Noah asked with a gleam in his eyes.

"Of course, but why wait?" Sherry asked.

"Because we're picking Quinn up after this, and she'll want to celebrate with us," Noah replied.

Sherry slapped her palm against her chest, her eyes going misty. "Oh, you are a good man." She squeezed his shoulder and then gave us our privacy.

I kind of forgot we were in a restaurant when I leaned up and kissed Noah. When I drew away, he murmured, "We do have an audience, you know."

My cheeks flushed. "I was already a scandal here. A kiss isn't going to make it any worse than getting pregnant when I was in high school."

He chuckled as I slipped off his lap and returned to my chair.

Later that night, we refused to let Quinn have any champagne. "Really?" she pressed.

"Yes," Noah said firmly.

"Let me see your ring again, Mom."

She sat at an angle across from me on the big sectional in the living room. The Christmas tree lights twinkled over by the bay window, and a fire flickered in the fireplace as I leaned over to show her the ring again.

She bit her lip, her gaze a little bashful when she looked up at us. "I love it."

"Thanks for giving Noah your blessing," I replied.

"Well," she said when she leaned back and brushed her hair off her shoulders with a flourish. "It was necessary. Now, I have a show to watch. Can I go upstairs?"

"Off to your room," I said, laughing when she leaped up from the couch.

Matilda followed her up the stairs. Noah had set up a TV for her in the guest room upstairs the last time we came here with her.

I leaned into his shoulder. "All that power is going to go to her head," I teased.

I felt his shrug, and then he leaned over to dust a kiss across my lips. "So what? I love you, you know."

I looked up at him, once again feeling the hot press of tears at the backs of my eyes. Apparently, having a man I loved ask me to marry him turned me into a water fountain.

"I love you too. Are you sure? I mean, I come with a teenage daughter included, and it's not always easy."

"I don't care how complicated it gets sometimes."

I fell asleep on Christmas Eve, thinking I couldn't quite believe my luck. Waking up on Christmas Day, one year after our first week here together, was too good to be true. My old hometown, which I'd run from as though my very self was on fire, leaving my scandal in my wake, had become my favorite place to visit. We'd already made new memories. We had more to make this year.

I hurried down the stairs, my smile almost an ache of joy when I found Noah in the kitchen making coffee. "Merry Christmas," he said as he turned.

. . .

Thank you for reading Noah & Sasha's story - I hope you loved it!

Up next in the Haven's Bay Holiday Series is All We Have.

Ian & Jane find themselves stuck together in Haven's Bay when a winter storm blows in. Jane was the quiet, book-ish girl in high school. Ian was popular and paid so little attention to his little sister's friend that he barely recognizes her.

Maybe he didn't recognize Jane, but now Ian can't keep his eyes off of her. Being trapped in the house with her only fans the flames of his desire.

Don't miss Ian & Jane's story - a swoony, opposites attract, snowed-in story!

Pre-order All We Have - due out Nov 15, 2022!

For more swoony romance...

This Crazy Love kicks off the Swoon Series - small town southern romance with enough heat to melt you! Jackson & Shay's story is epic - swoon-worthy & intensely emotional. Jackson just happens to be Shay's brother's best friend. He's also *seriously* easy on the eyes. Shay has a past, the kind of past she would most definitely like to forget. Past or not, Jackson is about to rock her world. Don't miss their story! Free on all retailers!

Burn For Me is a second chance romance for the ages. Sexy firefighters? Check. Rugged men? Check. Wrapped up together? Check. Brave the fire in this hot, small-town romance. Amelia & Cade were high school sweethearts & then it all fell apart. When they cross paths again, it's epic - don't miss Cade's story!
Free on all retailers!

For more small town romance, take a visit to Last Frontier Lodge in Diamond Creek. A sexy, alpha SEAL meets his match with a brainy heroine in Take Me Home. Marley is all brains & Gage is all brawn. Sparks fly when their worlds collide. Don't miss Gage & Marley's story!
Free on all retailers!

If sports romance lights your spark, check out The Play. Liam is a British footballer

who falls for Olivia, his doctor. A twist of forbidden heats up this swoon-worthy & laugh-out-loud romance. Don't miss Liam & Olivia's story.
Free on all retailers!

FIND MY BOOKS

Thank you for reading All I Need! I hope you enjoyed the story. If so, you can help other readers find my books in a variety of ways.

1) Write a review!
2) Sign up for my newsletter, so you can receive information about upcoming new releases & receive a FREE copy of one of my books: http://jhcroixauthor.com/subscribe/
3) Like and follow my Amazon Author page at https://amazon.com/author/jhcroix
4) Follow me on Bookbub at https://www.bookbub.com/authors/j-h-croix

5) Follow me on Instagram at https://www.instagram.com/jhcroix/

6) Like my Facebook page at https://www.facebook.com/jhcroix

———

Haven's Bay Holiday Series

All I Want - free on all retailers for the holiday season 2022!

All I Need - release date Nov 1, 2022

All We Have - release date Nov 15, 2022

All We Are - release date Nov 29, 2022

Light My Fire Series

Wild With You

Hold Me Now

Only Ever Us

Fall For Me

Keep Me Close

With Every Breath

All It Takes - coming Jan 2023!

Dare With Me Series

Crash Into You

Evers & Afters

Come To Me

Back To Us

Take Me There

After We Fall

Swoon Series

This Crazy Love
Wait For Me
Break My Fall
Truly Madly Mine
Still Go Crazy
If We Dare
Steal My Heart
Into The Fire Series
Burn For Me
Slow Burn
Burn So Bad
Hot Mess
Burn So Good
Sweet Fire
Play With Fire
Melt With You
Burn For You
Crash & Burn
That Snowy Night
Brit Boys Sports Romance
The Play
Big Win
Out Of Bounds
Play Me
Naughty Wish
Diamond Creek Alaska Novels
When Love Comes
Follow Love
Love Unbroken

Love Untamed
Tumble Into Love
Christmas Nights

Last Frontier Lodge Novels

Take Me Home
Love at Last
Just This Once
Falling Fast
Stay With Me
When We Fall
Hold Me Close
Crazy For You
Just Us

ACKNOWLEDGMENTS

I meant to expand this story, oh, three years ago. Sasha & Noah's story was percolating in my brain back in 2017 when I wrote All I Want - the first story in the Haven's Bay Holiday Series. Life and other stories got in the way, so I wrote a much shorter version that was included in a holiday anthology in 2019. My grand plan was to expand it and release the full version the following year. So much for that. More life and more stories and a worldwide pandemic slowed me down. Now in 2022, drumroll... the full version of their HEA is here!

Much gratitude to my readers for asking me for more stories in Haven's Bay and for reading *any* of my stories! Thank you, thank you, thank you!

Gracious thanks to my editor and to Terri D. for being the detail queen for my stories. Yoly Cortez created the gorgeous covers for this series and gave them the dash of holiday magic they needed. My author world would be a lot more topsy-turvy without the help of my assistant, Erin.

Hugs to my early readers and to the bloggers and book lovers who share my books and those of many other authors. Your love of romance makes the world a better place!

Last, but never least, to DBC and my dogs. You are my home and my heart.

xoxo

J.H. Croix

ABOUT THE AUTHOR

USA Today Bestselling Author J. H. Croix lives in a small town in Maine with her husband and two spoiled dogs. Croix writes swoony contemporary romance with sassy women and alpha men who aren't afraid to show some emotion. Her love for quirky small-towns and the characters that inhabit them shines through in her writing. When she's not writing, you can find her cooking, counting the turtles in her backyard pond, and running with her dogs, which is when her best plotting happens. Take a walk on the wild side of romance with her bestselling novels!

Places you can find me:
jhcroixauthor.com
jhcroix@jhcroix.com

 facebook.com/jhcroix

instagram.com/jhcroix

bookbub.com/authors/j-h-croix